BLACK
DIAMONDS

J. MICHAEL HERRON

ISBN-13: 978-1481965286
ISBN-10: 148196528x

To my wife Susan for her love, support, help and encouraging me to write

PROLOGUE

The quality time Meagan Turner had planned to spend with her Mom was not to be. Oh well, she thought, why should this turn out any different than anything else that had taken place in the last couple of years.

I'm only 29 years old and my life is already falling apart, she mused. I don't like the job I worked so long and hard to obtain. What little there is of my love life has evaporated. My Dad, who happened to be one of my favorite people in the world, died unexpectedly. And now when I was hoping to get away with Mom and escape all the turmoil and grief since Dad's death, the fickle finger of fate has once again intervened.

Meagan had booked a cruise to Alaska for her and her Mom, Helen, to share. Scheduled to depart in just four days, it had been her hope that the beautiful scenery and the time together talking and sharing would help ease the pain her mother had been feeling since the death of her husband of 33 years. Meagan had also hoped she could somehow regain the close, trusting relationship the two of them had shared before she went off to college. Now her mother's pending foot surgery and the required post-surgery hyperbaric treatments had turned those plans upside down.

To top it all off, she hadn't purchased the insurance the travel agent had suggested she add and at this late date could not cancel the trip without forfeiting the more than $6,000 she had already paid for the weeklong cruise and post-cruise tours of Denali and the Kenai Peninsula. Despite the fact she was single and earned a good income, she could not in good conscience justify throwing away the money even if she did have a comfortable nest egg set aside. Besides, her vacation time was set and the accounting firm for which she worked had already brought in temporary help for the three weeks she had scheduled off.

Helen had, of course, suggested that Meagan go ahead with the plans and find a friend to accompany her. What a sad state of affairs, thought Meagan, that for the life of me I can't think of anyone else I'd like to have go with me and share the experience. There hadn't been a man in her life of any significance since Richard had angrily called it quits and stormed out of her condo a little over a year ago. And if the truth was known, she hadn't been all that sorry to see him go. She had neither sought nor run into another male since in whom she was interested. And most of the women she knew were more professional acquaintances than what she would consider friends.

She had spent most of her time since college building her career as an accountant, something that consumed far more than the sixty hours she logged weekly just in the office alone. The hobbies she enjoyed and the friendships she had had in college and high school had largely been relegated to the back burner as she had determinedly pursued her goal of becoming a partner at McClary & Burns, one of the premier accounting firms in San Diego. Now that goal was in sight. That she had been successful in obtaining it only four years after leaving graduate school came as no surprise to anyone who knew her. Meagan usually got what she set out to achieve.

So why did she now feel so empty inside? Was it just a natural depression setting in after her Dad, who had given no previous signs of health problems, suffered a heart attack at work and died? That was part of it to be sure but somehow she knew there was more. She had been less and less satisfied with the direction her life was taking for a couple of years if she was honest with herself. Somehow she was losing touch with a critical part of who she really was, even if she couldn't clearly put her finger on what was missing.

It wasn't not settling down and raising a family, although that figured prominently in her plans for her future as well.   She had wanted to first obtain a partnership so she had the wherewithal to pay for a nanny and other childcare expenses while she continued her climb up the career ladder and secured her financial future.   She still had a number of years to bear children ahead of her.   Of course, it would help if she had someone with whom to share the creation and rearing of these imaginary children.

Sighing, she once again scanned the contact list on her MacBook Pro.   Who did she know who could rearrange schedules on such short notice?   Perhaps more importantly, who did she know with whom she'd like to spend a week cruising and another week in hotels in Alaska?

After working her way through the majority of her contacts she zeroed in on Diane Taylor.   Diane had been her roommate during her last three undergrad years at UCLA.   Diane had majored in psychology while Meagan studied business.   The two had become fast friends sharing the usual college experiences and then their paths had diverged as Meagan pursued a career in finance and Diane focused on law figuring it offered a better income potential.   Since school they exchanged an occasional phone call and sent holiday cards, but they hadn't gotten together in person.   After law school Diane went into private practice in Palm Desert, a small, rural community in Southern California. If memory served Meagan correctly, Diane had two other attorneys in the practice. Perhaps she could free up the time. But would she want to might be a better question.

Naturally she was put through to Diane's voicemail after dialing her cell phone. Meagan left what she hoped was an enticing message about a 2 week all expense paid Alaskan cruise tour vacation if Diane could manage to leave in just 4 days. She also stammered out an excuse for not calling sooner but would explain when they talked. Satisfied she had done what she could Meagan hung up the phone.

Diane called back in less than an hour. After some preliminary catching up including bringing Diane up to date on her Dad's death, Meagan got to the heart of the matter. "I scheduled a vacation for my Mom and me to relax after my Dad's funeral and winding up his affairs. It was my present to her and I never considered she'd end up needing foot surgery and treatments afterwards that precluded her ability to travel. Now I have flights to Vancouver and back from Anchorage scheduled, a balcony cabin booked on the Coral Princess, and accommodations at the Kenai Princess Lodge and Denali Princess Lodge the week after the cruise. Since I didn't purchase trip insurance it's now a use it or lose it situation."

"Count me in. I can reschedule the appointments I

have during the first week or get others to fill in for me. However I have to be back right after the cruise because I have two trials scheduled the following week and those can't be postponed."

"Let me give the airline a call and see if I can switch my Mom's ticket into your name. I'll be back in touch as soon as I've heard."

Meagan contacted the airlines and for a modest change fee was able to substitute Diane for her Mom and change Diane's return date to a week earlier so she'd be back in time for her trial dates. Meagan left her own itinerary unchanged and figured she'd make any decisions about it later. She called the cruise line and did the same for the cruise. She then called Diane and let her know the arrangements. They talked briefly about what to wear and possible excursions to take. Meagan sent copies of the flight schedule and cruise itinerary via email so Diane could pore over them in more depth at her leisure. They agreed to meet at the airport in Vancouver, Canada and take the transportation arranged by Princess Cruises to the ship.

Next she called her Mom and let her know she would indeed be moving forward with the vacation plans as scheduled. "I'm glad to know you will be getting away as I've been concerned about how hard you've been working," was her Mom's response. "It seems to me you need to do something fun just for the sake of enjoying yourself. Post some pictures on Facebook and give me a call when you have some time. And don't worry about me. Your sisters will hover over me throughout the procedure and take care of anything I may need afterwards. Just relax and have a good time."

With her next few weeks rearranged in a way that would have surprised her only a few days ago, Meagan silently contemplated her new plans as she packed her clothes and other things needed for a trip to Alaska. Despite all the unexpected changes she looked forward to getting away and breaking her established routine.

CHAPTER 1

A blue sky greeted Meagan with the promise of a beautiful May day as her flight landed in Vancouver shortly after 11 am on Saturday. After collecting her luggage and going through customs she went to the International Reception Lobby to await Diane whose flight was scheduled to arrive only 20 minutes after hers. While waiting she wandered over to the Princess Cruises Information desk to reconfirm their shuttle to the ship.

Diane's flight was on time and she saw Meagan immediately as she entered the International Reception Lobby. Her former roommate's dress tended to be more proper and true to form she was attired in Pendleton pants and sweater complemented by black knee high boots. Although only 5' 2" in height, Meagan had long legs and the outfit showed them off to perfection. Her long brown hair had a hint of red that was subtly picked up by the colors in the outfit. While in college she had effortlessly maintained a weight of 110 pounds and to Diane's appraising eye nothing had been added since. Upon catching sight of Diane a wide smile replaced the harried look Meagan had been wearing and the two embraced.

"Thanks for agreeing to join me on such short notice Diane. I hadn't realized how much I missed being together until I saw you now. How do we manage to get so caught up in day to day stuff and neglect what is really important?"

After filling each other in on how their flights were they both agreed to postpone any further serious discussion until they were settled in their cabin and sharing a glass of wine. Luggage in tow they headed to the gathering site for the Princess shuttle and in less than a half hour they were wending their way through the embarkation process. A short time later they were on board.

The majority of the staterooms on the Coral Princess had ocean views. Meagan and Diane found their balcony cabin on the Baja deck and quickly unpacked. Situated on the starboard side of the ship they would be afforded spectacular views as the ship made its way north towards Whittier. Room service was called and a bottle of Cabernet Sauvignon ordered.

Since it was mid-afternoon and the sun was shining brightly, they adjourned to the balcony to talk and catch up while the ship finished preparations for its voyage.

Meagan was amazed at how quickly she had opened up and unloaded the things that had been bothering her. It must have been festering for longer than she had realized. Or maybe it was the two glasses of wine she'd already consumed that loosened her tongue. She rarely had more than a glass because she didn't like it when her head started to spin. She didn't feel any lightheadedness from what she'd had so far, perhaps it was because of the appetizers they'd had with them. Or maybe she was just finally getting things out in the open where they could be looked at.

When the two had been college roommates they would often sit and talk for hours on end. They had discussed everything from classes to life goals to the male species. They had shared their first sexual encounters and the excitement and confusion both had experienced. No subject had been off limits and few had been skipped. It felt easy and natural to slip back into that mode.

To her credit, Diane simply absorbed all the frustrations and insecurities Meagan verbalized. She occasionally asked questions for clarification but mostly she just listened.

"I thought I had it all mapped out. Get career established. Find someone to share things with. Build a future together. Travel. Have fun. Buy a house. Raise a family."

"So what happened?"

"I'm not sure. I'm on track to become the youngest female partner in the firm's history by the end of the year. That pretty much takes care of the financial security. But that's all I've managed to accomplish since leaving school."

"Isn't there anyone in your life?"

"Not since Richard and I broke up. Since then I just can't seem to find the time, inclination or energy to put into building a relationship."

"Why did the two of you split?"

"It just got so boring and predictable. We were both building careers and that consumed a huge amount of our time. We had professional obligations that took up most evenings. It reached the point where we had to schedule time to be together in our calendars. Tuesday evenings were the only weeknight available and even then it had to be after 8 pm. Saturday evening we'd get together again and at least have through Sunday. If one of us had to travel out of town even those times might be gone. I mean what kind of relationship is it when you have to pencil in the hours to spend together just like it was a business appointment?"

"Did you love him?"

"I thought I did. I wanted to. But now in retrospect I'm not sure I ever really did. I think I was more in love with the idea of being in love."

"Why did you first get together?"

Meagan thought back. She had met Richard at a meeting of San Diego area financial planners. He was building a career as a securities trader. They had talked shop for a while and commiserated about how boring the meeting was they were attending. Before the evening ended he had asked her to dinner the following weekend. One thing led to another and they began seeing more of each other. When they finally went to bed together it was pleasant and tender. Sometimes he'd stay at her place and occasionally she'd stay at his. It was all very tidy and convenient. But it seemed like everything they did together centered around jumpstarting each other's careers. She finally confronted him about what they were doing and where they were heading and what it all meant. He seemed surprised she wasn't as content as he was and became defensive. They argued about it for a week and then he was gone. Her initial reaction was now she had more time available in her schedule. The problem was she didn't know what to do with it.

"I guess it felt like something I should be doing to keep my career moving forward."

And that, she realized, is a pretty sad reason to have as the basis of a relationship.

The ship left dock and began its northward voyage. Engrossed in conversation the two barely glanced up and did not join the crowds on the Lido deck for the bon voyage festivities. When they chilled from the breeze as the ship picked up speed they adjourned to their cabin. A second bottle of wine and some sandwiches were ordered. Their discussions continued.

"Well, if it's any consolation to you I can't say my love life and career are doing any better than yours."

Surprised, Meagan looked up. In college Diane had always had to beat off the men. Physically, the two could not have been more dissimilar. Where Meagan was brown haired and brown eyed, Diane had blond hair and blue eyes. At 5' 10" Diane had always towered over her. Ample cleavage and sensual curves contributed to the feeling you had just encountered a Norse goddess. And this surely must have been an advantage in the courtroom where any normal man would find himself unable to concentrate on matters at hand. Meagan suddenly had a surge of hope that she wasn't alone in the world.

It turned out not all was roses in Palm Desert either. Although firmly established in her law practice, Diane was experiencing doubts about whether a successful and profitable career was enough to keep her motivated to put in the long hours required. And despite no shortage of want-to-be suitors, no one had maintained her interest for long and none had captured her heart. She owned a nice house and drove a nice car but both seemed empty somehow.

"That's why I found it so easy to rearrange my schedule to go on the cruise when you called. I was desperate to get away and figure out what I need to do next. I don't know how much longer I can keep going the way I'm going."

Meagan was astounded. Where had all the dreams gone? In their college years both had been so completely sure the path they were pursuing would lead them to the happiness they sought. They had been successful on their chosen paths and yet here they both were feeling unfulfilled.

"So where do we go from here?" Meagan mused. "Do we just need to set new goals and start planning all over again?"

"I'm not sure," replied Diane, "but I don't think the answer is to sit down and logically and rationally outline my life. My parents instilled in me the need to approach things using logic. All the teachers and counselors throughout my academic life reinforced that method. Maybe it works for them but it doesn't seem to have worked for me."

Meagan pondered the response. Her parents had their share of financial struggles raising a family in the early years of their marriage and from them she had learned the importance of managing money and attaining financial security. Their house had been filled with love and caring but there was no question the approach to money had been calmly rational. While no one had ever gone hungry in the house the pennies were counted carefully and any considered purchase was calculated. She hadn't had many of the frills and extraneous things some of her childhood friends had but didn't feel that had necessarily been a loss.

There was no question that the approach to money she had learned at home had influenced her decision to pursue a career as an accountant. Math had come easy to her and while it might not have been her first love she was good at it. Plus the accounting field paid well, was projected to continue to grow, and was one that allowed her to choose where she'd like to live. So why couldn't she just accept that and be satisfied?

The concept of turning off her brain and following her heart was not a natural one for her. In fact, had anyone asked, she would have told them it was not a good way to make decisions. Up till now she had followed her brain in making decisions and look where it had gotten her. At a crossroads where she felt stuck and unable to move forward. So how did she break the cycle? This was new territory for her.

The bottom line was she needed to take a different approach and make some changes in her life. So what was holding her back? She knew for sure she was uncomfortable with where she was. Was she afraid of failing? She supposed she was but she also knew she had failed so far in nurturing the feeling side of herself. Of course no one else could see that part of her she thought.

"Perhaps I just need to quit worrying about what others think and concentrate on what makes me feel good." Meagan wasn't aware she had spoken the words out loud.

"Makes sense to me," Diane replied. "But it also sounds like it's easier to say than to do based on what I've done to date."

The third bottle of wine was accompanied by individual servings of chocolate molten lava cake. Each decadent spoonful of the dark chocolate concoction brought sighs of bliss. And the pairing of chocolate and red wine was a match made in heaven. After scraping every last vestige of brown crumbs from her plate and licking her spoon clean for the second time Meagan contentedly sat back.

"Okay, that's it. I've decided. Beginning now you're going to see a new me." Meagan giggled as she tried to get up from the couch and found things to be a bit unsteady. "Guess I haven't found my sea legs yet." Using the wall for support she managed to make her way to the bathroom.

After she returned any attempts at serious conversation quickly vanished. The combination of wine and leaving their stress-filled worlds behind brought out a more playful side of both. They were soon caught up reminiscing about college days and shared experiences. Snorts of laughter intermingled with tearful remembrances as memories of carefree days were recalled. It was 1 am when they turned out the lights. Lulled by the movement of the ship they were quickly asleep.

CHAPTER 2

She was standing near a river, amid a scattering of pine trees set back a short way from the river's bank. Although it was the middle of the day the sky was dark as storm clouds moved rapidly overhead propelled by the wind. As she watched a raven flew towards her from the far side of the river. It was carrying something in its talons although from the distance she couldn't tell what it was.

A bolt of lightning lit up the sky and snaked its way down towards the ground striking a large pine across the river. The crack of thunder was instantaneous. A wisp of smoke arose from the tree and small flames could be seen.

When she looked up again whatever the raven had been carrying was no longer visible. The bird dove down to the shore and frantically flew in circles trying to locate its lost cargo. After several unsuccessful attempts it flew directly towards her. Its frenzied cry assaulted her ears as it circled her once and then flew back towards the shore. When she didn't move it repeated the process several times, each time amplifying its calls and its efforts. Finally it flew off into the distance.

As the rain enveloped her she looked up to the sky. She couldn't tell if the wetness on her face was from the rain or the tears streaming down her cheeks.

Meagan awoke with a start. She felt the dampness on her pillow and her face. What a strange dream she thought to herself. I wonder what it meant. Glancing at the clock she saw it was only 4 am as she turned over and settled in to an uneasy sleep.

CHAPTER 3

The first full day of their voyage after leaving Vancouver was spent cruising. Due to the length of their conversations the previous evening, plus the wine consumed, they both slept in, skipped breakfast, and later had a leisurely lunch in the Bordeaux dining room. Even though the weather was partly sunny the breeze produced by the ship's forward progress was chilly so they decided to stay indoors for the time being.

They found lounges on the Lido Deck near the Lotus Pool in a glass-enclosed area that allowed them to see the scenery through the floor to ceiling glass without being exposed to the elements. Meagan shared her dream of the raven with Diane. "It was the strangest thing. This big black bird just kept circling around me and cawing up a storm. It did it over and over almost as if it was trying to tell me something.

And when it left there was the most incredible sense of sadness." She shook her head and laughed. "Maybe I just had too much wine, or maybe not enough. I don't remember ever having a dream like this before."

They spent the remainder of the afternoon exploring the Coral Princess and its offerings. They attended a presentation outlining activities available the following day and found their first choice still available. They played bingo without success. They had selected the anytime dining option and meandered into the dining room around 6 pm. After dinner they decided to skip the shows and nightlife scene and make it an early evening since they were scheduled into port early and their tour departed shortly after arrival.

The Coral Princess docked in Ketchikan precisely as scheduled at 6:30 am. They took the coffee and bagels room service had delivered and stepped outside onto their balcony as they came into port. They marveled at the maneuverability of so large a ship as the thrusters were able to gracefully and smoothly move the ship sideways until it gently came to rest against the pier. The day was overcast and damp so they had donned windbreakers over sweaters and jeans.

The beautiful town of Ketchikan is located 679 miles north of Seattle on the western coast of Revillagigedo Island, near the southernmost boundary of Alaska. The historic downtown is wedged between water and forested mountains. It is built into steep hills and partly propped on wooden pilings, dotted with boardwalks, wooden staircases and totem poles. The name of Ketchikan supposedly derives from the term "Katch Kanna" which roughly translates to "spread wings of thundering eagles." It is aptly named for you only need to look along the water line to see numerous bald eagles on waterfront perches.

For their first port excursion they had chosen to tour the Saxman Native Village to learn about the culture and history of the Tlingits, the original inhabitants of the lands they were visiting. They made their way down to the disembarkation deck, inserted their Cruise Cards in the machine to record their exiting the ship and joined the rest of their tour group on the dock to await the bus that would transport them to their destination. The ride was a brief one and they soon found themselves admiring the totems and the native dancers as they learned of the history.

Saxman Native Village was named after Samuel Saxman, a Presbyterian teacher who was lost at sea with a Cape Fox elder while searching for a new school and church site. It is known for its large collection of Native American totem poles and, in fact, has the largest collection of standing totem poles anywhere. Inside the carving house they watched as totem poles commissioned from all over the world were created by hand. Inanimate objects are forbidden on poles and all carvings represent living beings. The Tribal House was traditionally used as a communal facility for several clans or families and in it they saw totem poles telling their history.

As they browsed the shops located in the village Meagan was approached by one of the women in a store offering small totem figures as souvenirs. She was asked if she knew her animal totem. Upon confessing she had no idea she was asked several questions and then instructed to look through a series of photographs to see if any of them in particular called to her. Several photographs of bears captured her attention, particularly one of a mother and her two cubs fishing in a river. The woman nodded as she watched the process unfold and confirmed that based upon what Meagan had shared the bear was indeed her totem. Meagan purchased a small wooden bear and put it in her purse.

After leaving the Saxman Native Village Meagan and Diane wandered along Creek Street peering in the storefronts. Before long they found themselves at the Tongass Historical Museum. Paying their entrance fee they went in and were drawn to one of the permanent exhibits entitled The First People – Tlingit, Haida and Tsimshian Heritage. A sign announced a storytelling scheduled to begin in just a few minutes. They made their way into the small auditorium and found seats in the front row. An elderly shaman attired in native garments sat cross-legged on a stool facing the audience.   He focused his gaze on Meagan for a moment before launching into his tale. His voice was captivating and his delivery rhythmical.

"Today I shall share with you why the salmon return from the sea – the legend of the raven and the heart of stone.

A very long time ago a Tlingit tribe lived along the banks of a large river near where it flowed into the ocean. Kamiro, the chief, had a headstrong daughter named Aliana whose totem was the bear from which she received her will power, courage and great strength. Her beauty was unrivaled and had garnered the attention of many young men throughout the region. Kamiro wanted to promise her to the son of a neighboring tribe's chief to strengthen ties between the communities.   But Aliana had fallen in love with Yakuzo, the son of a fisherman in her own village.

'Father, I want to marry the one I love. I wish to bear his children and live a life filled with happiness and joy among the people I know and cherish. I do not want to leave our village to live somewhere I don't want to be with someone I don't love.'

Yakuzo's totem was the salmon and while proud and confident he also exhibited the wisdom and inspiration associated with it. He and Aliana frequently walked the riverbanks and the sea's shore engaged in intense conversations as their relationship deepened and grew.

It came to pass that the villagers were hungry for this had been a lean year for both crops and hunting. Yakuzo and a number of other young men set out to sea in search of salmon to feed the village. The fish were far offshore and the trip would require a journey of many days.

Kamiro sent a runner to the neighboring village with instructions for the chief's son to come at once and be betrothed to Aliana. The chief's son quickly left in anticipation of finally being able to be with the one whose beauty had so captivated him. As he prepared to cross the river to Aliana's village she caught sight of them. She quickly figured out her father's plans and ran from the village into the forest.

She summoned a raven, and sent it winging out to sea to seek out Yakuzo and tell him of her plight. The raven landed on the boat and relayed all she had confided to him. Yakuzo told the raven to pluck the heart from his breast and take it to Aliana as a symbol of his eternal love and to seal their engagement. When they next reunited she could return it to him and their love would be complete. The raven took his heart and flew off.

Night was approaching as the raven neared the

village. Black clouds had gathered and a fierce storm ensued. While dodging a bolt of lightning it lost its grip on Yakuzo's heart. The heart turned to stone the color of the raven's brilliant black feathers as it tumbled down to the riverbank where it buried itself among the rocks and boulders lining the river.

Without a heart, Yakuzo found himself confined to the nether world where he was destined to roam along the ocean and rivers waiting for his heart to be returned by the bear maiden so he could once again become whole and fulfill his pledge of love.

Overcome with grief Aliana never returned to her village. She remained in the forest and when the winds blow the sounds of her crying can be heard in the trees. On stormy nights it is said she can be seen along the banks of the river searching for the heart of her lost lover.

That is why when the salmon returns to the river from its journey to the sea he finds the bear waiting for him. She is searching for both the heart and her salmon lover so she can free him from the spirit world, their love can become complete, and they can be reunited once again.

And that is also why to this day black diamonds may be found along the rivers and streams of Alaska."

After concluding his tale the shaman arose from his

seat. His pace was slow as he approached where they were sitting and took Meagan's hand in his. He examined her palm before his eyes lifted to hers.

"When I saw you enter the room I was compelled to share with you the tale I told today. It was not the one I was asked to present. I would urge you to remember it well and take it into your heart for it speaks to your future."

Releasing her hand he turned and slowly shuffled out of the auditorium. Meagan and Diane looked at each other without speaking, both wondering what had just happened. After a few moments they left the museum and made their way back to the ship.

The Coral Princess departed Ketchikan at 2 pm. They spent part of the afternoon attending a presentation on shore excursions available the following day in Juneau and decided to visit Mendenhall Glacier. After that they returned to the Lotus Pool area, reclaimed their previous lounges, and watched the scenery pass by. Little was said about the mystical encounter with the shaman in Ketchikan as they both seemed content to mull it over internally.

They went to dinner early and then attended the evening's performance featuring Broadway show tunes in the Princess Theater. Both were impressed with the quality   of   the   entertainment   and   applauded enthusiastically.   After the show they stopped for a nightcap at the Wheelhouse Bar and listened to the piano player perform.   They then returned to their room and called it a night.

CHAPTER 4

She found herself standing beneath a pine tree beside a river. It was still daylight although the sun was working its way down the sky and shadows were beginning to form. As she watched a man walked along the river's edge. He was tall with brown hair and a lean build. He was casually dressed in a blue chamois shirt and tan cargo pants. He appeared to be lost in thought. She silently continued to observe him as he knelt by the water, inserted his hand, and seemed to be searching among the rocks. As if suddenly aware of her presence he turned toward her and lifted his head. His features seemed both rugged and gentle at the same time. A short brown beard ringed his face. But it was his eyes that captivated her. She had never seen eyes such an intense blue. It felt as if two blue laser beams were aimed directly at her, boring into her. Without a word he arose and began walking towards her. She thought about fleeing but her feet seemed rooted to the ground. His eyes never left hers as he approached.

Meagan opened her eyes. She was still in her bed in her cabin on the Coral Princess. In the bed next to hers Diane continued to slumber. So what had all that been about? Her heart was still racing and her breathing rapid and shallow. Was she losing her mind with all these strange things going on in her head? Last night's dream she could at least rationalize because of the wine. Maybe she was having a breakdown. That would explain it. After she got back to San Diego she'd schedule a full checkup. Turning over, she tossed and turned for a while and then fell back asleep.

CHAPTER 5

The following morning greeted them with a brilliant blue sky. Even with full sun it was cool and both Meagan and Diane donned sweatshirts and windbreakers. Breakfast in the dining room consisted of lox and bagels, juice and coffee. Fortified for the morning they adjourned to their balcony to watch the docking in Juneau. When the process was completed they walked down the stairway and joined the throng of people leaving the ship. The bus ride to the Mendenhall glacier took less than a half hour and they were dropped off at the visitor center.

Mendenhall glacier extends 12 miles from the Juneau ice fields, its source, to Mendenhall Lake and ultimately the Mendenhall River. Originally named Aak'wtaaksit ("the Glacier behind the Little Lake") by the Tlingits it was renamed in 1891 in honor of Thomas

Corwin Mendenhall who was responsible for defining the exact national boundary between the United States and Canada.

During a brief tour of the center they learned about glaciers. They found out the orange (long wavelengths) part of white light is absorbed by the ice while the blue (short wavelengths) light is transmitted and scattered. The longer the path the light travels in ice the bluer it appears. The purity and age of the ice also play a factor in the color of ice in glaciers. As the ice ages it is compressed, melted and frozen again eliminating air bubbles that scatter the light rays and bounce them back out again in the same color they came in (white). Once the ice becomes pure the light waves are much more likely to be absorbed promoting the deep blue color.

Armed with their newfound knowledge they walked out the East Glacial Loop trail to an overlook providing unobstructed views of the glacier. The dazzling sun reflecting off of the pristine white ice was reminiscent of the sparkle of diamonds. Both of them snapped pictures with their cell phones.

"Wow! Have you ever seen such an intense blue?" queried Diane as they rounded a corner and were afforded a close-up view of the glacier.

"Yes," Meagan thought to herself silently, "I have.

I saw it last night in a stranger's eyes. That blue put these glaciers to shame."

"You know," she said aloud, "these colors are truly stunning. I'm going to buy a good camera and start taking pictures of all this scenic beauty we keep encountering."

"In school you used to be really in to photography. And painting. Why is it you haven't maintained that interest? You were really talented at both."

"Just one more of the things that fell by the wayside as I focused on my career. I think it is time to rekindle my outside interests once again."

The bus returned them back to the area where their ship was docked.

"I don't want to go back onboard yet," said Meagan. "Let's stroll downtown and look around."

They headed down towards the Red Dog Saloon, recognized as the oldest man-made tourist attraction in Juneau. It was reputed that in territorial days a mule would meet tour ships at the docks with a sign that said "follow my ass to the Red Dog Saloon."

As they walked down Franklin Street Meagan spotted a camera store, The Digital Express. She went inside and inspected the cameras available. Some $500 later she emerged with a new Sony CyberShot DSC-

HX200V digital camera that featured a 30X optical zoom and all the accessories she needed, including a carrying case, 32 gig memory card and a spare set of rechargeable batteries.

"I guess I'm going to get re-interested in photography," she offered lamely. "At least I have the equipment now to start doing that."

As they emerged from the camera store she looked across the street towards the Red Dog Saloon. A block down from it she spotted The Bear's Lair. Instead of going to the saloon she found herself entering the store that specialized in Native American art and artifacts.

A young woman with long black hair pulled back in a ponytail greeted her. "Can I help you?"

"I'm not sure. Something told me I'm supposed to be in this store right now," she stammered. "I think it has something to do with this," she said as she pulled her bear totem from her purse.

"Grandmother, I think this person wishes to talk with you," the clerk called over her shoulder.

Meagan watched as an ancient and wrinkled woman arose from where she had been sitting. She had seen the woman as she had entered but had honestly thought she was a mannequin sitting so still against the wall. It surprised her to realize that this was a real live person.

"My name is Shawana," the woman said. Her voice crackled and sounded as old as she appeared. Her skin was as brown and wrinkled as a walnut. "May I ask what brought you to this place at this time?"

"I honestly don't know. I just saw the name, The Bear's Lair, and knew I had to come here. I'm supposed to learn something but I don't know what."

The old woman nodded, concealing her own astonishment. She knew that now, in the autumn of her life, she was supposed to pass on something she had been carrying with her since she was a young woman. Yet she had never thought it would be given to someone who was not of her tribe. But she also did not doubt the prophecy foretold.

"What is your totem"?

"The bear."

"And what are you seeking?"

Meagan contemplated the question. She wasn't sure what she was looking for. She knew she was looking for something but had never specifically thought about what it might be. She was far too logical to respond flippantly, but she didn't know what was expected of her. The words that came from her lips surprised her.

"I am in search of love, happiness and knowledge. I wish to bring peace and closure to a place from which it has been lacking for a long time."

The old woman nodded sagely. She turned and muttered some words in a language Meagan didn't recognize to the young woman who had greeted Meagan when she entered the store. The woman bowed to the old lady and retreated to the back of the store. When she returned in a short while she carried an object that she handed to the old woman who reverently accepted the package.

"My totem is the raven. We of the raven totem were given this charge because of the role played by the raven in losing the lover's heart. I received this from another raven woman. It was given to her by another before her and by many others before that. I had always thought I was to pass it on to another of my clan but now I find it is to you it must be given."

She handed the package to Meagan. Something was wrapped in sealskin. When she unwrapped the skin she found a hand hewn cedar box. When she opened the box she found a walrus tusk yellowed with age. The box had been lined with fur to hold the tusk securely in place. Etched on the tusk was a scene depicting a river with pine trees lining its banks flowing from the mountains to the sea. A jet-black raven carved from stone arose from the middle of the river. Its wings were spread as if in flight and something was clutched in its talons. On either side of the river, flanking the raven, were figurines of a bear and a salmon. Both had been carved from walrus teeth and they, too, were yellowed.

"This talisman has been passed down through generations awaiting a bear woman seeking love and fulfillment as only she will have the capabilities necessary to fulfill the prophecy," the old woman said. "It is said that when the time comes she who is its current guardian will know what to do."

"And what is the prophecy?"

"Two lovers are waiting to be made whole and united. For that to occur a bear woman must commit acts requiring great courage and unselfish love. And she must give her heart freely to a salmon man who will assist her. When that has taken place the lovers will be together at last and she who helps bring this about will find a path leading to her true destiny. If you accept this I will have played my part in fulfilling the prophecy."

"Why are you giving this to me?"

"You are a bear woman and you came inquiring about the bear totem. And you are seeking enlightenment. It was foretold."

"I accept the obligation." Meagan was amazed to find herself answering. "And I will do everything within my power to fulfill the prophecy."

"If you but follow your heart and it is destined to happen it will be so. Should it not, you must find another bear woman seeking the same and pass it on to her."

"I understand."

CHAPTER 6

Without speaking Meagan and Diane made their way back to the Coral Princess. Once they were onboard and in their cabin, Meagan placed the talisman on the stand beside her bed. She sat and stared at it. Then Diane started in.

"What just happened back at that store? This is really out there."

"I know, and I don't have a clue as to what's going on. I've always been so logical and rational. I've never believed in myths and superstition. I'm struggling to think that there may be more to this than I've considered."

Meagan then added to the confusion by sharing with Diane the dream she had the night before and the man she met with eyes the color of the deep blue they had seen in the glacier that day. Neither could fathom what all these strange experiences might mean.

Meanwhile the Coral Princess continued her northward journey.

The next day brought rain. Because it was so wet and windy neither of them left the ship while it was in Skagway. While Diane watched a movie and went to the spa for a massage and pedicure Meagan contented herself with becoming familiar with her new camera. She read the manual and took numerous pictures. One of the nice things about the digital age is you can simply try different things and then erase any results you didn't like. The box and talisman had been put in their room safe although she would occasionally get it out and look at it before returning it for safekeeping. She found that if she kept herself occupied learning the details of her camera that she didn't have to think about the strange things taking place in her life.

The final two days of their voyage would be spent cruising Glacier Bay and College Fjord. In preparation for what they would see they attended a lecture by an Alaskan naturalist. He informed them that Glacier Bay, the body of water, covers an area of 1,375 square miles, accounting for 27% of the area of Glacier Bay National Park. It started out as a large single glacier of solid ice till early in the 18th century. It then began retreating and evolved over the centuries into the largest protected water area park in the world. The original Grand Pacific Glacier was about 4,000 feet thick and 20 miles wide. Over the past 200 plus years it has retreated by 65 miles to the head of the bay at Tarr Inlet, and in this process left separate 20 other glaciers in its trail.

He told them before reaching Glacier Bay they would cruise past Lituya Bay located in a remote part of Glacier Bay National Park. On July 9, 1958 an earthquake triggered a landslide that caused 30 million cubic meters of rock and ice to fall into the narrow inlet of the bay. The sudden displacement of water resulted in a wave hundreds of meters high that washed over trees and was ultimately measured as washing 1,720 feet up the opposite slope of the inlet, 470 feet taller than the Empire State Building. This is the highest known mega-tsunami and the largest known in modern times. The wave possessed sufficient power to snap off all trees up to 1,720 feet high around the bay. Most of these were spruce and many were over six feet thick. The wave stripped the soil down to the bedrock around the bay. There were three fishing boats anchored near the entrance to the bay on the day the giant wave occurred. One boat sank and the two people on board were killed. The other two boats were able to ride the waves. Survivors provided written accounts of what they observed. Based on the length of time it took the wave to reach the boats after overtopping Cenotaph Island near the bay's entrance, the wave was calculated to have traveled up to 600 miles per hour. When it reached the open sea, however, it quickly dissipated. This incident was the first direct evidence and eyewitness report of the existence of mega-tsunamis.

The weather the next day cooperated and blue skies and bright sunshine prevailed. At this time of year daylight came early and stayed late. Meagan was captivated by the spectacular landscapes that kept flowing past the ship, particularly the glaciers. She took picture after picture, experimenting with different settings and functions of her new camera. She managed to capture a wall of ice plunging into the water as one of the glaciers calved. The mountains were the most rugged she had ever seen rising straight up out of the ocean thousands of feet reaching for the sky above. Trees clung tenaciously to sheer rock faces seemingly impervious to the elements and blissfully unaware of their precarious position.

The ocean was teeming with life. She saw birds, otters, seals, walrus, whales and even a pod of Orcas. Bears roamed the shorelines while eagles perched on branches in the trees alongside. They would periodically take wing and glide effortlessly on invisible air currents while they scanned the waters below for their next meal. Everywhere she looked there was something new to see. And everything was duly captured as her finger kept pushing buttons and her eye seemed glued to the viewfinder. Periodically she'd go inside and transfer her most recent images to her MacBook Pro. She'd swap out her camera batteries for fresh ones and put the used ones in the charger.

She wondered why she'd ever stopped doing this, indulging in something that pleased her so much. She could hardly wait to get on her computer and start playing around with the pictures to sharpen them up and create the effects she desired. She knew she had gotten some really good shots to begin with and with a little work could turn them into something great. This was a side of her that she'd neglected for too long and she resolved not to let it happen again.

The final night of the voyage arrived almost before she knew it. She and Diane hadn't talked as much since the incident in Juneau. It was almost like they were both processing things independently, waiting to see what would come out of it. Tomorrow they would dock in Whittier and Diane would take the train to Anchorage and her flight back to California. Meagan was scheduled to board a bus taking her to the Kenai Princess Lodge to begin the land portion of her trip. After three nights there she would head to the Denali Princess Lodge before flying back to the Lower 48.

They were in their stateroom packing suitcases to be set outside their door for pickup and delivery to their next destinations. Meagan had retrieved the talisman from the safe and put it in her carry-on bag so she'd have it with her at all times.

"So you're going to stay up here by yourself for the next week. Is that the plan?"

"Yeah, I just feel like it's something I'm supposed to do. You know, it seems like for the past few years I've found myself swimming upstream against the current. It's really hard to make any headway and not only that but it's a lot of work. I'm tired and I'm tired of fighting it. I think that for a change I'll just relax and see where it is this river is so determined to take me. This is pretty heady stuff and a real change for me."

"I know it is. Do you think you'll be all right?"

"I'll be okay. I mean I don't feel like I'm in any danger or anything like that. This is just such a new experience. I don't think I've ever just gone with the flow before. I've always known where I was heading."

"Well, like I've always said. Life is what happens after you make plans."

Meagan laughed. "Isn't that the truth? Just when you seem to get comfortable someone throws you a curve. So what are you going to do?"

Diane pondered the question a moment before answering. "I don't know. I think this time together has helped me finally realize that I'm going to have to make some changes in my life. I guess when it's time to do it I'll do it. At least now I feel like I have some energy to get through the next round."

The following morning after their last shipboard breakfast they found themselves in the debarkation lounge with many others. When Diane's group who would be going to the Anchorage airport was called, they stood and gave each other a hug.

"Thanks so much for coming. If you hadn't agreed to come with me I doubt if I would have made the trip. And it's been so good to rediscover our relationship. It's very important to me. Your friendship means a lot."

"Same here. Give me a call when you get back."

Diane turned and luggage in tow headed off the ship. Meagan sat back down and awaited the call for the bus ride to the lodge. When it came she dutifully followed the group and boarded the bus.

CHAPTER 7

David Solomon was frustrated. Even though he had abandoned the mainland corporate world to create a more relaxed and personally fulfilling lifestyle in Alaska it seemed he constantly encountered the need for political posturing in his efforts to get even a small business off the ground.

At 32 years of age I'm already becoming a dinosaur, he thought. The reality was, despite his current state of mind, he was far from a fossilized creature. He and two other classmates had managed to leapfrog the field and create a billion dollar internet business within five years of leaving his college days at the University of Southern California. David managed to stick it out for a couple more years but finally gave in and sold his interest after helping take the company public. What he had discovered about himself during the process was while he could get excited about taking an idea and bringing it to fruition, he had little interest in maintaining it once the creative period had passed.

At one time he had entertained the idea of a future in professional basketball. Although only 6' 2" he was an accomplished athlete and had developed into a high scoring shooting guard for the Trojans. During his junior year he had averaged 25 points per game and was being courted by several pro scouts. As luck would have it on his way to dunking a fast break layup he had collided with an opposing player and his off-balance fall had shattered his right knee and ended any dreams of a basketball future. In his senior year he found he could channel his competitive nature into the planning of the business he later co-founded.

After selling his portion of the business, he found himself taking stock of his current situation, where he wanted to go, and what he wanted to do. He was well off financially and had managed to weather the economic meltdown that had affected the stock and real estate markets, largely due to his Dad's solid advice on investing a significant portion of his resources in precious metals and foreign currencies. While he enjoyed traveling and exploring new places and people, he knew himself well enough to realize he would soon have to find something tangible into which to funnel his time and energies.

Like many young boys before him, David had once fantasized about becoming a forest ranger. He had first been exposed to nature during camping and hiking outings as a Boy Scout. It was a far cry from the suburban environment of the San Fernando Valley in California where his childhood was spent. Then, on a trip with his Dad celebrating the sale of his business, he had rediscovered his love of the outdoors. They had gone salmon fishing at Hakai Pass in British Columbia and the fishing was surpassed only by the majestic scenery. He found he could comfortably spend hours surrounded by water, trees and mountains.

A subsequent trip to Alaska and its awe-inspiring natural wonders found him down on the Kenai Peninsula and the quiet little town of Homer. It was here he found the tranquility and beauty he craved. He bought a house in the hills above Homer with panoramic views of the snow-capped mountains across Kachemak Bay. He spent his first summer traveling throughout Alaska from Juneau in the south to Nome in the north. He went east to Denali and Fairbanks. But he always looked forward to returning to Homer, the place he now considered home.

It was while walking on the Homer Spit and talking with a group of somewhat disenchanted tourists that an idea for his project began to percolate. The tourists were staying at the Best Western Inn and trying to figure out where they should go and what they should see in the four days they had allotted to spend in the area. While the staff at the Best Western were friendly enough, their suggestions were geared primarily towards traditional tourist attractions and activities when what they really wanted to do was see the real Alaska.

May through September traditionally brought large numbers of tourists to the area for fishing, wildlife viewing and simply to enjoy the scenery. What if he put together a kind of one-stop shop for people who really wanted to get to know the Alaska he cherished. They would need a place to stay, food and a way to experience the unique beauty and activities the 49th state had to offer. Most people who spent the kind of money to get all the way here in the first place wouldn't hesitate to spend a little more to get the kind of experience they really wanted.

The more he thought about it the more excited he became. This was something he could really sink his teeth into. He would find a place on the hills surrounding Homer that provided panoramic views of the bay and the snow-capped mountains across it. On a clear day perhaps they would even be able to get a glimpse of the volcanoes on the northern Alaska mainland. It needed to be large enough to accommodate enough people to make it economically viable yet small enough to make you feel that this was a comfortable piece of the Far North that had been created especially for you.

Gourmet meals would be prepared from fresh Alaska ingredients that would satisfy the most discriminating palate. All meals would be included in the package, even going so far as to pack 5 star picnic lunches to consume on the excursions available. A wide and diverse menu of activities would be available to enable guests to create their own personal Alaskan experience.

David pulled out his cell phone and called his father, Ralph, a general contractor in Southern California. Although he started out building houses nearly 30 years ago, Ralph's primary focus the past few years had been developing and building condominiums and resorts. "Hi Dad. I have something I'd like to run by you if you've got a moment."

"I always have time to listen to what you have to say, son. Go ahead."

David quickly outlined his thoughts on what he'd like to create.

"Sounds like it just might fill a need for something different for visitors. Why don't you start putting some numbers together and thinking about what kind of property you will require. See what's currently available. It would cost less to modify something than to build from scratch. Should be a good time to buy with the down economy. The types of people you're hoping to attract always have disposable income available so you should still be able to line up enough business to make it work. Let me know when you've narrowed down some options and I'll come up and help you figure out the best alternatives."

That had been nearly two years ago and the concept for Alaskan Adventures, LLC had been born. A twenty-acre piece of land on a hilltop overlooking Homer was purchased. A large log home that already existed had been converted to the common area and housed the living quarters for the primary caretakers. In addition to the dining area there was a large lounging area that included a full wall of books featuring a section on Alaska and its varied offerings. Behind the scenes was a commercial kitchen, walk in freezer and pantry, and commercial laundry facilities.

Twelve cabins had been constructed surrounding the main building. Each had been positioned for the best view yet had a sense of privacy due to being scattered among the small pine trees that dotted the property. Covered porches for each cabin featured comfortable rocking chairs and a hot tub. Inside were a bedroom, bath and a lounge area that included a mini-fridge to maintain a supply of beverages. A table and chairs for in-room dining, a sofa convertible to a queen bed, and two overstuffed chairs comfortably positioned for reading and scenery gazing comprised the main furnishings. There was wi-fi throughout the property but the only television was located in the main lodge. Guests were here to pursue their Alaskan dreams not to remind themselves of what they had chosen to leave behind.

A large garage had been constructed capable of holding not only vehicles driven by the guests but those of the staff. It was connected to the main house by a covered walkway. A separate building housed maintenance and recreational vehicles and equipment. The overall effect was one of rustic elegance and had been christened Kachemak View Lodge.

David had been fortunate enough to locate and secure the services of the perfect people to manage the place. Carolyn Clayton had been the Assistant Manager at the Alyeska Resort in Girdwood and her husband, Jerry, had been the chef at the Seven Glaciers Restaurant there. Together this team brought both a wealth of experience, contacts and skills necessary to transform Kachemak View Lodge into the kind of environment David had envisioned. They were handling all the details of the day-to-day operations, including overseeing the housekeeping, maintenance and dining staff.

One of David's roles was to promote the facility and negotiate contractual arrangements for the various tours and activities from which guests would select as they personalized their Alaskan experience. Their grand opening was coming up soon and many details still remained to be finished. While he appreciated and valued the rugged individuality that characterized Alaskan entrepreneurs he silently cursed them for their casual approach to business arrangements. On the flip side of the coin was the "Lower 48" mentality whereby people who wanted to run their operations just as they had in the big cities they had left felt they were stooping down to a level that was beneath their station. This particular dynamic had created his current frustration.

"Yes, I'll hold for Mr. Thompson. I'm sure he has many demands on his time and I appreciate his taking a moment to talk with me." David was trying to convince the Kenai Princess Lodge manager to allow guests of Kachemak View Lodge to be included in some of the outdoor activities available to Princess guests including gold panning and upper Kenai River guided fishing. It would be a win-win because they could jointly generate a larger number of clientele that would in turn ensure their referrals received a higher priority from the tour operators. He figured if they sent a lot of business to someone that they would in turn be more amenable to customizing the offerings as necessary to better fulfill customer wants and desires.

"Hello Mr. Thompson. David Solomon here. I sent you a proposal two weeks ago on how we might collaborate on certain activities to the benefit of both of our respective clientele. Have you had a chance to review it yet?"

Thompson acknowledged he had in fact received the proposal although he had not yet gotten around to looking at it. "If you could make the time to read through this I'd appreciate it. Perhaps I could come by this afternoon and discuss it with you. Yes, I'll schedule an appointment with your secretary. Thanks for your consideration of my request and I'll see you in a few hours." He hung up the phone and sat back in his chair. He sighed as he felt the beginnings of a headache coming on.

CHAPTER 8

The Kenai Princess Lodge sat perched high atop a bluff overlooking the turquoise waters of the Kenai River in Cooper Landing, the site of the first discovery of gold in Alaska in 1848, one year before the California Gold Rush. Although rustic in appearance it featured first class amenities and accommodations.

Meagan checked in and found her way to the outlying bungalow she had originally planned to share with her Mom. The bungalow featured a cozy sitting area with a wood-burning stove thoughtfully stocked with wood and kindling that only awaited being lit. A covered front porch featured rockers from which you could gaze down on the river below and hills beyond it.

Since there would be no one to occupy the other double bed she used it as a table and deposited her luggage and other items on it. Her talisman went into the in-room safe. She set up her MacBook Pro and started to resume work on her pictures. Changing her mind she returned to the main lobby and went to the tour desk to see about scheduling some activities. She picked up some brochures as well as a map of walking paths and trails in the vicinity and decided the day was too nice to remain indoors. Returning to her room she changed into comfortable walking clothes, grabbed her camera and set out on the path leading down to the river.

The path wound its way through the trees as it descended to the river. It was secluded and peaceful down here. The only sound breaking the tranquility was the murmur of the water as it flowed towards Cook Inlet some 75 miles away. She took some pictures of the clear blue water backed by the green trees on the opposite shore. There was a large flat rock along the river's edge. She climbed onto it and sat there basking in the sun. From here she could look back up and see the lodge. She took a couple of pictures of it as well.

As she prepared to step down the sunlight glinted off of something near the base of the rock. She got down on her knees for a closer look. There, she could see a smooth shiny object just under the surface gravel and sand. She carefully brushed things off. What she found took her breath away. It was a small black rock shaped like a heart. She picked it up, rinsed it off in the water, then dried it with her handkerchief and held it in her hand. The luster was remarkable, in the bright sun it shone like a black mirror. It was so perfect it looked like it had been formed and polished by a machine. She wrapped it in her handkerchief and placed it in her camera bag. Standing up, she headed towards the path leading up to her cabin.

When she got back to her room she retrieved the talisman from the safe. She placed it, the small wooden bear totem she had purchased, and the stone heart on the table and stared at them. What in the world is happening, she thought. Have I fallen down a rabbit hole to find myself in Wonderland? This can't be real. Yet these things are solid and tangible. Where is this path I'm on taking me? And what is next?

She put everything in the safe and went to the main lodge. She went into the gift shop where she found a small leather pouch with a drawstring. The pouch held a few tiny samples of local minerals. She purchased the pouch, together with a silver chain, and returned to her room. Opening the safe she removed her bear totem and the heart. She removed the mineral samples from the pouch and tossed them in the trash. She replaced them with the stone heart and her bear totem. She attached the pouch to the silver chain and put it around her neck, tucking everything beneath her sweatshirt. She needed to have this with her while she figured out what is going on. I believe I could use a glass of wine, she thought, and headed out to the main lodge.

CHAPTER 9

David's discussion with Mr. Thompson had gone as well as could be expected he supposed. They would try a working arrangement for the next several months and see where it went from there. Thompson actually had some good ideas on how to improve on David's original suggestions and his secretary would be typing up those changes for him to take back with him to Homer. Since it would take a couple of hours before she could get those completed he thought he'd go over to the bar and have a beer.

When he entered the Rafter's Lounge Meagan was just picking up a glass of wine and heading out to the deck to enjoy the scenery. Now that is an attractive woman, he thought, as he went up to the bar to order a beer. With his glass in hand he chose a seat where he could watch her sitting on the deck. She looks preoccupied, he thought.   I wonder what's going through her mind right now. Doesn't she know people come here to be on vacation and forget their cares?

It had been a while since there had been a woman of any significance in his life. That wasn't because some hadn't tried as he had received a number of inquiries and invitations from a variety of women after helping take his company public. But he wasn't looking for someone to help him spend his newfound wealth. Call him old-fashioned but if he was going to put forth the time and effort necessary to build and maintain a relationship he wanted it to be for love. And to date he hadn't found anyone to fill that bill. Right now his time was filled with trying to get Alaskan Adventures off the ground. He couldn't afford to lose his focus if he wanted that to succeed. And he did.

Despite the fact he told himself he wasn't really interested he found himself looking at her again and again. There was something about her that called to him. He could feel a pull. He wouldn't say she had movie star looks but she certainly was attractive and easy on the eyes. It was more in the way she carried herself and what her body language conveyed. Her bearing was regal, that was it, kind of like a modern day Audrey Hepburn. When she entered a room people would notice. He would bet she wasn't even aware of the effect she had on men. But it was there, he could attest to that.

He wondered what it would be like to kiss her, to taste her, to hold her close and feel her slender body pressed tight against his. He wanted to feel her heart beating against his chest. Would it speed up? His was speeding up even as he contemplated this. Why am I doing this to myself? She's probably here with her husband or a boyfriend who just happens to be someplace else at the moment. It was rare for a single woman who had her looks to travel alone in Alaska. Men significantly outnumbered women here and a woman like her would have a lot to choose from.

In the short time he had been watching three men had approached and spoken to her. She had quietly but firmly declined their invitations and they had returned to their seats.

Whatever was on her mind continued to bother her. He could tell it from the way she'd gaze off into the distance without seeing what she was looking at. She drank the last sip of her wine, stood up from her table and left the deck, apparently going to her cabin.

David finished his beer and looked at his watch. He still had a good hour before the papers would be ready for him to pick up. He decided to walk down to the river for a while to escape the noise that was picking up as more people filled the lounge. He paid for his beer and left.

CHAPTER 10

Meagan returned to her bungalow and sat on the edge of the bed. She pulled the pouch from beneath her sweatshirt and emptied the contents into her hand. Both the heart and the bear were about the same size, perhaps an inch long, maybe a little less. She wondered what else was going to happen during the balance of her trip.

She had enjoyed the glass of wine but had wanted to be alone with her thoughts. The bar scene wasn't for her and she didn't want to have to fend off any more men who wanted her attention. It had all been politely handled and they hadn't been persistent but it intruded on her concentration. Maybe she'd just go back down by the river to where she had found the heart. In that solitude she could get back to her thinking and figure out what she needed to do next. She put the items back in the pouch and put it back on under her sweatshirt. She walked out the door neglecting to bring her camera.

She neared the bottom of the trail and remained among the trees. Someone was already down here. She didn't want to share this spot with anyone else. It was hers. Didn't this man know that? She watched as he gathered some flat pebbles and stepped up on the big rock where she had sat. He threw a couple of them, trying to see how many times he could make them skip. Apparently his windbreaker was holding him back because he shrugged out of it and tossed it casually behind him on the shore. To her astonishment he was dressed in a blue chamois shirt and tan cargo pants. It was the man from her dream.

CHAPTER 11

David felt rather than saw her back under the trees. He threw the remaining rock he held and watched it skip several times before sinking beneath the surface of the water. He turned to face her and stepped down from the rock on which he'd been standing. He watched her face as he walked towards her. She remained motionless like a deer caught in the headlights.

He stopped when he was directly in front of her. To her credit she had not turned and run. He reached out his arm and gently traced the outline of her face with his fingers. He could feel heat where his fingertips touched her skin. He moved closer, leaned in, and lightly brushed her lips with his. He pulled his head back and looked in her eyes. She gazed back without fear although he thought he saw a flicker of excitement.

He put his hands on her shoulders, pulled her to him, and kissed her again. This time he deepened the kiss and was rewarded with a small moan. He felt it when she abandoned any resistance and eagerly added her own efforts. He felt her arms encircle his neck. This was more than he had anticipated or imagined. It was far more powerful and intense than any kiss he had ever experienced. He broke off the kiss and allowed his lips to explore her face, her ears, her neck. He inhaled her scent and tasted her skin. She sighed and molded her body to his.

He drew back and looked at her again. He tried to take in every single detail of her face. How could he have not originally thought her beautiful. She was magnificent. He found he wanted to explore her completely, all of her.

She looked back at him, holding his gaze. Suddenly she smiled and her face lit up. It felt like a bolt of lightning had just struck him. Looking up at him she uttered the first words of their encounter. "If I'd known this was how you welcomed a woman to Alaska I would have been here a lot sooner."

He smiled back, his eyes never leaving hers. "I just aim to please, ma'am."

"Well trust me, you please very well. Very well indeed."

"I wanted to do that from the minute I first saw you walk out to the deck up at the lodge. And it was even better than I thought it would be."

"I'm glad you weren't disappointed."

"Anybody who would be disappointed with that is either beyond hope or already dead."

She smiled again. "My name is Meagan Turner."

"Pleased to meet you, Meagan. I'm David Solomon."

"Come here often?"

He laughed. "I didn't before but I surely plan to do it more now."

"Well I thank you for that." She said, accepting the compliment. She gently disengaged herself from him but kept his hand in hers. "Would you walk with me up to my cabin, please?"

He retrieved his windbreaker and they strolled up the path together comfortably and companionably. The conversation was light and effortless. He stopped several times to point things out in the surroundings that she hadn't noticed before. When they reached her cabin she let go of his hand and turned to face him.

"I'd be lying if I said I hadn't been thinking about

inviting you in to continue what we started but I just can't do it right now. I'm sorry."

"Don't be. I'm not sorry at all. But I think it's only fair to let you know I want you although I'm sure you've already figured that out."

She nodded and he continued. "I can be patient and I will. But I know at some point we will get together." He smiled wryly. "Confidence is a hallmark of my totem – the salmon."

She staggered back as if he'd just struck her. Concerned, he gathered her in his arms and deposited her in the chair on the porch. "Meagan, what's wrong? What happened? Are you okay?"

"It's nothing. Oh, hell, it's everything. I don't know. Or maybe I do." She knew she wasn't making any sense but she didn't know how to make sense out of what was happening, what she was feeling.

She composed herself and looked up at him. "David, I need to sit down and talk with you. I don't want to do it right now. I need some time to think first. I have to figure this out." Her eyes pleaded with him, silently imploring him to understand.

"Why don't I come back tomorrow around noon. We can grab some lunch and talk."

"Thanks for understanding. And thanks for being

so kind."

"It's all part of the service, ma'am." He smiled, then turned and walked away.

CHAPTER 12

Meagan continued to sit on the porch looking off into the distance. After a few minutes she got up and went inside. It was cool but not particularly cold but she lit the fire anyway. She just wanted the comfort it afforded. She pulled up a chair and sat staring as the fire came to life. The movement of the flames was hypnotic and she found the warmth and crackling sound emitted soothing. She removed her sweatshirt and absentmindedly fingered the leather pouch.

It was all happening so fast, she thought. Everything seemed unreal. Her life had always been structured and orderly with everything tucked into its proper compartment. Nothing about this fit that mold.

She had been stunned when he discarded his jacket and she saw the man from her dream. When he fixed those blue eyes on her she had felt unable to move, even if she'd wanted to. And she hadn't wanted to move. That had surprised her. She wasn't afraid and nothing about the way he walked up to her had been threatening. Instead it had almost felt familiar, but how could that be. They had never met before except in her dream. Or had they?

When he'd touched her face she'd sensed a connection with him. She couldn't explain it but she'd definitely felt it. When he'd first lightly kissed her she'd been somewhat amused that he would take her so for granted. She held back wanting to see what would happen. The second kiss, when he circled her lips with his tongue then darted it inside, it was as if a window to her soul had been opened. She'd been powerless to resist, completely caught up in the heat she felt, and she'd responded by pulling him closer, immersing herself completely in the kissing and feeling.

If he'd pulled her to the ground with him then she'd have gone willingly. Of that she was certain. But he hadn't. Instead he'd just pulled back and looked at her. It wasn't that he didn't want her she knew from his eyes he'd wanted her. She suddenly realized he had been giving her the chance to decide for herself what she wanted to do rather than forcing himself on her. She was grateful for that, she decided. And her respect for him went up a notch.

Tomorrow will be interesting, she thought, as she drifted off to sleep by the fire. Despite her trepidations she found herself looking forward to it.

CHAPTER 13

The drive back to Homer was uneventful. At least what little David could remember of it. It was as if he'd been driving in a fog. Thank God for doing things on autopilot because his mind certainly hadn't been on what he was supposed to be doing. And fortunately the traffic had been light and no stray moose had wandered into his path.

When he'd turned and saw her standing in the trees it was like a siren was calling to him, one he was powerless to resist. His feet had seemed to move as if they had a mind of their own and he couldn't stop looking at her. And she looked right back at him just as intensely.

She hadn't shied away when he'd touched her. It was as if she had known of it beforehand and had prepared herself. And the power he'd felt when they truly kissed. She'd felt it too. He could see it in her eyes and hear it in her breathing. He'd wanted to possess her right then. And he could have, he knew. But something had held him back. There was more to this than met the eye. So he'd retreated and given her the option. When they'd walked up the path he'd thought she would invite him in.

What was it he'd said while they were standing in front of her cabin? She'd turned as white as a sheet and he thought for a minute she was going to faint. He'd caught her before she could fall. He'd watched her struggle to compose herself. Then she'd said they needed to talk. And she'd pleaded with him to understand and to give her some time. And he'd agreed. So tomorrow they would talk. But he was damned if that would be all they'd do.

Now he had to rearrange his schedule to spend time with her. As if he didn't have enough to do trying to get everything up and running in the business. But a part of him was curious at the same time. No, it was definitely more than curiosity.

CHAPTER 14

The next day was one of those spectacular ones you only encounter occasionally on the Kenai Peninsula. The sky was so blue it took your breath away. Pine needles still coated with morning dew sparkled in the sunlight like shimmering green diamonds.

As he drove to Cooper Landing David realized again how fortunate he was to have found this place. It reached into his very being and grabbed hold. As long as he had this everything else would take care of itself.

Meagan couldn't believe she was having so much trouble deciding what to wear. I mean this was Alaska, for heaven's sake. Everyone dressed casually around here. David had certainly done so yesterday. He wasn't going to dress up. She finally selected a pair of jeans and a green sweatshirt she had purchased in the lodge

gift shop that had Kenai Princess Lodge in writing and
a picture of a bear emblazoned on it. Might as well go
all the way with this totem thing she thought. Her bear
totem and the stone heart hung around her neck in the
pouch tucked under her sweatshirt. A pair of walking
shoes completed the ensemble.

She had purchased a small daypack as well and it
now contained her camera, sunglasses, a brush and her
windbreaker. As an afterthought she had retrieved the
talisman and put it in. Might as well let him see the
whole crazy package. Promptly at the stroke of noon
her room phone rang. He was in the lobby of the
lodge. She looked in the mirror and fussed with her
hair for at least the twentieth time. Slinging her
daypack over her shoulder she went to greet him.

He watched from his chair as she came into the
lobby and saw him. A smile formed on her face as she
crossed the room. "Thanks so much for coming,
David. It means a lot to me to have you do this. I
wasn't sure you'd actually come after all. I mean it isn't
often you encounter a crazy woman in the bush." She
stopped sensing she was babbling like a lunatic. Maybe
she was.

He just smiled back and said her name. Suddenly
she felt a calmness begin to descend over her and knew
everything would be okay. She could trust him. And
he would understand. At least she hoped he would

because she surely didn't.

He asked if she'd like to eat in the restaurant at the lodge.

"No. I took the liberty of asking the people if they'd prepare a lunch for us to take out. I hope I wasn't being too presumptive. I really need to talk with you and I don't want it to be in a public place where others can overhear. Do you know someplace we can go?"

"That I do if you don't mind a short drive."

"I don't. It's a gorgeous day out."

They retrieved the hamper from the Eagle's Crest restaurant. David hoisted it up giving it an appraising look. "Doesn't feel like we'll starve."

"I was hungry. I didn't know what you might want so I think I got a little of everything. They'll probably have to resupply the kitchen."

He laughed and took her hand. They walked out to his Jeep and he opened the door for her before putting their lunch in the back. He got behind the wheel and closed the door. He put the keys in the ignition but before starting the engine he turned to her, took her face in his hands and kissed her. It was gentle and soft but still filled with passion and, to her surprise, an intense longing. His tongue explored her lips and mouth. He sighed and released her. She sat there watching him.

"I wanted to do that. No, I needed to do that. I had to prove to myself that last night wasn't a dream. It wasn't. It definitely wasn't. Now let's go have our picnic and talk."

"Where are we going?"

"A little town called Hope. It's back a little ways towards Anchorage and sits off of the Seward Highway."

"I think I saw a sign for it when I rode in on the bus yesterday."

"Yes, you would have passed by the turnoff."

"Why do they call it Hope?"

"The town was originally settled by gold miners. The story has it that in 1889 they had decided their little community needed a name since it was growing so fast. After a lot of talking and no agreement someone made a suggestion to name it after the first person that stepped off of the next ship. His name was Percy Hope and the rest is history."

She chuckled. "Sounds like a very appropriate name for a town built around prospecting."

"They got most of their gold out of Resurrection Creek that flows into Turnagain Arm. There's a campground and some picnic tables there. Should be pretty quiet and we should be able to find a private spot."

They lapsed into a comfortable silence, each lost in their own thoughts. Soon they found themselves at the picnic area. They located a table in the sun alongside the creek. There was very little breeze and the murmur of the creek provided a nice backdrop. David carried the hamper over and Meagan started laying out the food.

"I hope you like wine. Other than water that's all we have."

"Wine's good with me. Want me to open it?"

She handed him the wine opener and the little chiller holding the wine bottle. When he opened it and removed the bottle he laughed out loud. She looked over and laughed as well.

"Pretty good, huh? When I looked through the wine list and saw one named Conundrum I figured it was meant to be. If this isn't some kind of puzzle or mystery I don't know what is. It just called out to me and I had to choose it. I don't know if the wine is as good as the name but we'll find out."

The label read Conundrum 2010 California White Wine. Like the naming of Hope it somehow seemed appropriate. He opened the bottle and filled two glasses. He placed them on the table and gazed appreciatively at the repast laid out. For appetizers there was smoked salmon, brie and crackers. The entrée sandwich was a croissant stuffed with smoked turkey, cream cheese and cranberry sauce. To polish it off there were strawberries, grapes and chocolate chip cookies.

They took seats across from each other. David raised his glass to her. "Here's to Hope."

"And to mysteries," Meagan added quietly.

They swirled the wine, inhaled the bouquet and took a taste. It was amazingly good. When it first entered your mouth it had sweetness to it. When it went down your throat the sweetness had dissipated and a completely different aspect of the wine emerged. He was surprised because he normally preferred red wines. He complimented her on the selection. They took their time working their way through the food and made small talk. He learned she was an accountant and both lived and worked in San Diego. This year she would make partner. He knew that was no small feat for a woman of her young age even in today's supposedly enlightened world. He shared his plans for Alaskan Adventures, the Kachemak View Bed &

Breakfast, and how much he enjoyed turning an idea into reality. It was comfortable talking with each other and neither seemed in a hurry.

When he had finally eaten all he could he gazed at the remaining food and reluctantly pushed himself away from the table. He suggested they go sit under a tree near the creek to talk. He topped off their wine glasses and helped pack the remaining food back in the hamper. He put the hamper in the back of his Jeep and retrieved two folding chairs he had brought. Meagan brought her daypack and the two glasses of wine and they settled in their chairs.

CHAPTER 15

She sat for a moment thinking of what to say and how to say it. Finally she turned towards him.

"You are going to think I'm crazy. At this point I'm not sure whether or not I am."

"Try me, Meagan. You might be surprised."

So she did. She told him of her father's unexpected death and how that seemed to be the start of a chain of events that disrupted everything in her life. How she started questioning everything she was striving to attain. She shared her mother's grief and how profoundly it affected her. How she had scheduled a trip to Alaska for the two of them to get away and let both of them heal. Tears formed in her eyes as she recounted this and David had to hold himself back from wanting to hold her and comfort her. He sensed that wasn't what she needed at this point.

She told him that when her mother needed care she couldn't back out of the cruise without forfeiting the money she'd already paid. She told him of getting her friend Diane to accompany her instead.

"And where is Diane now?"

"She could only come for a week. She's an attorney with her own practice and has trials going on."

"So you decided to continue by yourself. Pretty gutsy."

"I suppose it was. Or is for that matter. It's certainly out of character for me to be this spontaneous."

He waited, sensing she wasn't finished. She took a deep breath and plunged in.

"I haven't even gotten to the good part yet. That all started when I got on the ship."

She recounted the conversation she and Diane had the first night of the cruise and how the need to change things had crystallized for her. She shared her failed attempts at relationships. She told him of her dream of the raven. How she had discovered the bear was her totem at Saxman Native Village. How the storyteller at the museum changed his tale when she came into the room. She recanted the tale of the two lovers and how one lost his heart and had it turned to stone.

"That night I had another dream. I was down by a river when I saw a man wearing a blue shirt and tan pants. When he looked at me I felt as if I had been pierced by blue laser beams. I saw you, David, there by the river in my dream. That's why I didn't turn away from you yesterday. How could I when I had already dreamed about you? I woke up from my dream before I could kiss you but I knew it was going to happen."

She looked at him for reassurance. He really was a good listener. It didn't seem like he was passing judgment on her nor was he sending for men in white coats. So she continued and told him of her visit to the glacier and rediscovering her passion for wanting to capture memories in photos. How she bought a camera. How she stumbled into The Bear's Lair and came out with a talisman and an obligation. She removed the walrus tusk from her daypack and handed it to him. He examined it at length.

He started to say something. She held up her hand. "I'm almost finished. Let me get through it." She told him of her walk down to the Kenai River in the afternoon and how she had been on the very rock where she saw him that evening when she found the stone heart. She took it out of her pouch and handed it to him.

"I was confused and not a little bit frightened. This is all so strange. I was going back down to the river yesterday to try to sort it all out when I saw you. And you know the rest. I wanted desperately to cling to you last night but I had to try and sort it all out."

"And have you? Figured it out?"

"Not in the least. Any ideas?"

"Not off the top of my head."

He reconsidered a moment. He didn't want it to seem he had responded flippantly or facetiously. He knew this was weighing heavily on her mind.

"One thing I do know, Meagan. Just because I don't understand something doesn't mean I should disregard it. I believe things happen for a reason whether we know the reason or not at the time. I've never had the kind of mystical experiences you've described but I don't doubt they took place."

"So you don't think I'm completely crazy?"

"I think you're one of the sanest people I've ever met. I'd like to think I'd have handled myself half as well if all this had happened to me."

He tugged her gently from her chair and sat her on his lap. He pressed her head to his shoulder and just held her. He could feel the tension slowly ease from her body. They sat like that for a while, listening to the river, thinking their own thoughts.

She pulled back, looked at him and grinned. "So you think Conundrum was a good choice for the wine?"

He knew then she had relaxed from the tension he'd felt when he picked her up at the lodge.

"Oh yeah, I surely do. Maybe we'd better pick up another bottle or two. It seems we have a puzzle of our own to solve."

CHAPTER 16

The drive back to the Kenai Princess Lodge was relaxed and pleasant. Their conversation was light. After he'd parked she invited him to her room and he accepted. They dropped the hamper off at the café as they passed by. They picked up another bottle of Conundrum.

They opened the wine and took their glasses out to the porch. They sat quietly for a while admiring the view. Meagan finally broke the silence.

"You know a lot more about me now. I know next to nothing about you. Tell me about yourself. Where did you grow up?"

"Northridge which I guess means I'm a Valley Boy. I got a basketball scholarship to USC and thought I'd be headed to the pros. It wasn't meant to be. A knee injury removed that option permanently."

"How did you get all the way up here?"

Two of my classmates and I started a business right out of college. It did really well. But it reached a point where it wasn't fun any longer. After we took the company public I sold out and left. I bummed around for a couple of years before coming north and falling in love with the area. One thing led to another and here I am."

"Holy crap! You're that David Solomon, one of the members of the infamous Tech Trio. I read about you in Business Week. You're famous!"

"Yeah, well fortunately most of the people I associate with up here don't read business or technology magazines so I'm not that well known."

"Still, your folks must be proud of you."

"They are. My parents were divorced when I was four. My mother had an urge she never managed to really scratch and changed men like you'd change shirts. My sister and I spent most of our younger years with her going from place to place and man to man but I guess we cramped her style. I ended up being sent to live with my father and stepmother. I was 13 at the time. My sister was 15 and ended up getting pregnant and married. We both managed to escape using different means."

"Sounds like your childhood was pretty painful."

"It was I guess. It stabilized a lot when I went to live with my father. He was a big sports buff and was the one responsible for recognizing and developing my interest in basketball. I think having that outlet is what kept me going."

David rarely talked about either his mother or his childhood. He knew his rocky relationship with her and her numerous flings had hurt him, and hurt him deeply. He was sure it was the primary reason he'd never managed to maintain a serious relationship for any period of time. It wasn't that he didn't want one. He did. But for whatever reason he couldn't manage to let anyone in far enough to hurt him like that again. His father had remarried before he had gone to live with him. The two of them were devoted to each other and David's relationship with his stepmother was positive. But still he just couldn't seem to lower his guard and let anyone deep inside. Someday he would. It just hadn't happened yet.

"People don't always realize how their behaviors affect others, particularly kids."

"I've thought about that. In fact I've thought about it a lot. I don't blame my mother any longer. I realized she was just trying to be happy and live her life the best she knew how. You know, the things that happen to us are what shape us into who we are now. Mine aren't any better or worse than anyone else's. They're just mine. I have to figure out how to deal with them and move on."

"Sounds like the adult David talking. But the child David is still hurting."

Wow! Where did that arrow come from? She was right on. She saw right through him. He was going to have to be really careful around her. She could get inside pretty quickly. And he didn't want to be hurt any more. He sat for a while without saying anything.

"Are you close to your sister?"

"Yes, I am. Linda is a great lady. The guy she married was kind of a jerk and they ended up getting divorced. But she got two great kids out of the deal. She lives in Ventura. I keep in touch with her pretty frequently."

"And do you stay in touch with your mother?"

"We haven't talked in three years."

He got up and went inside and brought out the wine. He topped off their glasses, sat down and remained silent. Sensing his reticence to continue in this vein she shifted topics.

"So tell me about Homer."

His eyes lit up and he visibly relaxed. Homer was a slice of paradise. He shared with her the first moment he'd stood on a hill overlooking the city and seen the blue waters of the bay, the mountains on the far side, even glaciers were visible. He'd known then this is where he wanted to live. Like many Alaskan cities it had a small town feel, everyone knew each other by name, yet Homer had an upbeat side with the arts and crafts produced there. It was kind of like a miniature version of Carmel in California without the pretense.

He told her how when he was outdoors surrounded by unfettered nature, he finally felt at peace with himself and the world. It was such a powerful, even spiritual, sensation that he wanted others to be able to experience it. Which is why he'd created Alaskan Adventures. It was coming together but it just hadn't clicked yet, hadn't quite jelled. Most of the pieces were in place but he hadn't felt the soul of it yet that he so badly wanted to create. That wasn't quite right. He couldn't create the soul of it, all he could do was put the environment together and let the soul come of its own accord. The bottom line is he wanted to be able to give back to others what had been given to him.

"Given your background in finance and business, it probably doesn't sound like I'm much of a businessman with this project."

"On the contrary, I believe you can do well financially by doing good. The two aren't necessarily exclusive. In my experience most people only seem to zero in on the dollar aspect of an enterprise and forget the other. I tend to think that's a pretty short-sighted view."

"That's it exactly. When I helped build the internet business every decision was made with regard to how it affected the bottom line. If it didn't show there immediately it was discarded and something that would add dollars at once was substituted in its place. I found that it didn't matter to me whether we made a thousand dollars or a million dollars that day. What mattered was the long-term view about how we were affecting the people using our service. Did we enhance their life somehow with our products and services? Or did we merely separate them from their money. Don't get me wrong, I think money is nice to have. But what matters more is how you get it and what you do with it."

They sat on the porch, the silence comfortable between them. Meagan looked over at him as his eyes stared absentmindedly at the mountains across the river. He was ruggedly handsome. His eyes were the most intense blue she had ever seen. They had a lot of power when he focused them on you. Yet she had seen a glimpse of pain behind them as well. She found herself wanting to reach out to him, to touch him, to help ease the pain. Hadn't he done that for her when he had heard her out and then simply held her until everything had settled. How can I possibly be thinking about that? I'm only supposed to be in Alaska four more days and then its back to San Diego. But then what was all this mystical stuff? She looked at the mountains and let her mind wander.

David's mind, too, was hard at work. He glanced across at Meagan. When he had first noticed her in the bar there had been an attraction, he was male enough to recognize that for what it was. But when he had seen her near the river and held her and kissed her something had clicked inside him. Oh, there was the passion and the sexual stimulation to be sure. It was more than that. It was like she might be able to fill an empty spot inside of him. He'd known Homer was the place for him the moment he saw it and he wondered if Meagan was also a part of his destiny. Somehow that felt right. God knows he hadn't had a lot of success with relationships before. Would this be different? Could this be different? He didn't know, and that bothered him because he found himself wanting it to be different.

He looked at her intently until she turned to meet his gaze. She found herself holding her breath. He abruptly smiled and said, "So where do we go from here, Meagan? It seems to me we have unfinished business on a number of levels. We both want each other, that's clear to me. I want you in bed with me so badly I can hardly stand it. And I'll have you there at some point. But there's more to it than that, isn't there? There's this whole thing with reuniting ancient lovers and fulfilling a prophecy and whatever else may be involved in legends. I wonder how all that will play out."

"I'm scheduled to go up to Denali the day after tomorrow for three days and then fly back to my life in San Diego."

"Change your plans, Meagan. Cancel your reservation in Denali. Leave here now and come with me to Homer. I've plenty of room in my home although I'd hope we'd only need one room. Be that as it may, let me show you what I'm trying to build while we figure out the rest of it. That will give us four days and nights to figure out what we need to do next. I'm sure by then we'll both know what is meant to be."

He sat back and waited. He knew he'd issued both an invitation and a challenge. From the little she'd told him he was aware that acting spontaneously was not her style. But now the ball was in her court. She had to make the decision for herself. And he'd have to live with whatever decision she made.

Meagan pondered his request. She was astounded she was even seriously considering his offer. Here was a man she'd only known a little over a day and he wanted her to come stay with him for the next four nights. He had offered her privacy but he'd also made it clear he would welcome her company in his bed. She wanted to go to bed with him. And if she went with him it was inevitable that would happen. So what was stopping her? She mentally ticked off the pros and cons. On the surface it seemed there were more cons but that was because she was falling back on old habits and trying to solve this logically. And where had that way of doing things gotten her to date. What was it the old man in the museum had said? She must take things into her heart. And then the old woman who gave her the talisman had told her she must follow her heart. And her heart told her to go with David.

She looked David directly in the eyes. "In for a penny in for a pound. Help me pack and then I'll go to the front desk and let them know of the change in plans."

CHAPTER 17

Although it was nearing 10 pm there was still daylight when they arrived at David's house in Homer. They had turned off on Diamond Ridge Drive before entering the town and then driven along the winding road into the surrounding the hills. They turned off on a small cul-de-sac and drove to the end. The garage door opened and they drove inside.

"Come in the house and look around and then we'll come back and get your stuff."

Meagan was sure her jaw must have fallen to the floor when she entered the living area. On one side was a stone fireplace with the stonework reaching to the ceiling high above. The walls were a combination of cedar and sheetrock that had been painted to offer hints of color from the wood. The furniture was leather and wood that was both rustic and elegant. But it was the massive wall of glass and the view it provided that captured your attention. She thought it must have been thirty feet high at the peak and forty feet wide. Even on either side it still must have been ten feet tall as it sloped down. And when you looked through it, it was as if someone had painted a scene for a giant postcard. The town of Homer was visible below with the spit jutting out into the bay. In the distance snow-capped mountains framed the bay. The snow on the mountains was just taking on a pinkish tinge as the clouds prepared for their evening extravaganza. She stood by the glass and stared.

"My God, David. How do you ever manage to get anything done? I think I'd spend every waking moment just standing here looking out."

"Pretty awe inspiring, isn't it? I never get tired of it. And it's always changing, always different. I like it just as much when it's stormy and dark as when it's blue and sparkling."

She turned from the window and faced him. "Thank you for asking me to come here with you. I can't say I'm not a little nervous but I also know it's right for me and it's what I want and need to do for myself."

She put her arms around his neck and pulled him to

her. She found his lips with hers and probed with her tongue. It was like smoldering coals had been hit with a blast of wind and came fully to life. Her mind went blank as she was enveloped by sensations that were as new as they were exciting. All she could do was feel the heat and the promise of more to come. He took a deep breath and detached himself from the kiss. "Do you mind if we bring your things in later?"

"I think that's a fabulous idea."

CHAPTER 18

David scooped Meagan up in his arms and walked down the hallway leading to his bedroom. Opening the door he carried her inside. A king size bed covered by a white down comforter faced sliding glass doors leading out to the deck. The room rippled with muted reds, oranges and pinks from the spectacular sunset colors. He deposited her gently on the bed. His hands framed her face as he kissed her again. His lips moved over her face stopping briefly at her eyes, nose, ears, chin and everywhere he could find to kiss. He moved down and tenderly kissed her neck. He felt her shudder with delight.

He pulled back and tilted her head up. "I want to undress you and look at you, Meagan. I want to caress and ravish every inch of your body."

She merely nodded as she looked back at him. She found herself holding still, eagerly anticipating the next touch. He slid her sweatshirt from her arms and over her head, revealing the leather pouch. He unclasped it and placed it reverently on the nightstand beside the bed. He unbuttoned her blouse and pulled it back to reveal her shoulders and lacy white bra. He traced her throat and shoulders with kisses. He kissed her breasts through the bra pausing to lick briefly at each nipple that had already hardened.

He stopped to remove her shoes, her socks and her jeans. Only her panties and bra remained. His mouth resumed its journey down her stomach, legs and feet. She couldn't have moved had she wanted to. Everywhere his lips touched tingled as if a pleasantly light electrical current was stimulating each individual spot. Her body craved the sensations he was producing in it.

He unfastened her bra and removed it and her panties. She heard his sudden intake of breath. "My God but you are beautiful, Meagan. I had thought you were before but the reality of seeing you is overwhelming. You're like an exotic and erotic ivory sculpture. I need to feel you completely against me with nothing between us."

He quickly removed his clothes, discarding them carelessly on the floor. He lay down beside her and resumed exploring her body with his mouth. When he found her nipple and sucked it gently into his mouth she moaned and said his name aloud. His hand moved down and cupped her. She shuddered and arched upward against it as the first wave overtook her. When the quivers subsided he continued to stroke and knead her.

She soon found her feelings mounting again. "Take me, David, now. I want you inside of me. Please."

"I'll be there soon, I promise," he murmured. He pulled her body to his. She could feel his readiness and the heat he was generating. He lay on top of her and kissed her lips, his tongue parting them and penetrating inside. His hands continued to roam her body, caressing and soothing wherever they touched. He raised himself on his elbows and looked down at her. "I want to possess you, Meagan. I want to make you mine."

"Oh yes, David. Take me. Make me yours. Do it. Now." Her voice was fervent with desire. When he entered her, he felt her contract around him, arousing him even further. He slowly began to move and her body matched his pace.

"Watch me, Meagan. I want you to see me. See us." She opened her eyes and looked up at him. She saw the feeling in his face grow as his strokes grew longer and deeper. Her body responded in kind. When she thought she couldn't stand it any longer she felt him tremble as he emptied himself in her. He cried her name out as they went over the crest together.

CHAPTER 19

When he opened his eyes she was still in his arms, her body curled against his. The last vestiges of sunset were fading and the inky tendrils of darkness were creeping in. He didn't want to move, afraid to disturb the magic of the moment. The fact was, he wasn't sure he could move.

He was no stranger to sex but the intensity of what he had experienced had been completely unexpected. He had known from the first time they kissed he would enjoy making love with Meagan. What he hadn't known was he would lose control of his feelings in the process. He lived his life by controlling his feelings. If he didn't lose control he wouldn't be vulnerable. And if he wasn't vulnerable he couldn't be hurt. Yet he had just given up control. And he hadn't been hurt. He wondered what in the world he was letting himself in for.

She awoke to find her face against his chest. She inhaled his scent. It was warm and masculine and spicy. She felt his body touching hers and thought how well they fit together. She had certainly enjoyed what his body had done to hers. She thought she had never been loved so completely or so well. No, she knew it to be true. This was what she had always thought making love could be. It was as if her fantasy had finally come true. She hadn't known she was capable of feeling all the wonderful sensations she had experienced but there was no doubt she had felt them. And she was certainly glad she had. And she was glad she had changed her itinerary to visit Homer.

He felt her stirring. "Hungry?"

"Famished."

"I meant for food."

"That, too."

She snuggled even further against him.

"Let me display my culinary expertise first and then we'll explore the other."

He went to the closet and donned a pair of sweats and some running shoes. He retrieved a robe and slippers and handed them to her.

"These are a little big but why don't you put them on for now and we'll bring your stuff in after we eat."

"Let me use the facilities first and I'll join you in the kitchen."

She went into the bathroom. After using the toilet she stood in front of the mirror and ran a brush through her hair. She looked at her reflection. She didn't see anything but she knew something was different about her, she felt different. It felt good she decided. She went in search of David.

The kitchen was a chef's dream come true. A large granite island featured a cutting board and prep sink. Against the wall was a six burner Wolf range. An enormous Sub-Zero refrigerator and freezer completed the work triangle. The cabinets were a light oak with lighting beneath to illuminate the countertops. A coffeemaker gurgled and she could smell the aroma of the coffee brewing.

He looked up and noticed she was wearing her pouch around her neck. He smiled.

"How about an omelet, toast and coffee?"

"Sounds really good to me."

He expertly set about preparing the meal. He chopped and sautéed some onion, cooked and crumbled bacon, grated cheddar and mozzarella cheese.

He broke eggs into a blender, added a little milk and seasonings, and whipped the eggs until frothy. With butter melted in a frying pan he poured the mixture into it, covered it, and reduced the fire. He sliced thick slices of bread and popped them in the toaster.

"Can I set the table?"

"Sure. Plates and cups are in the cabinet on your left. Silverware is in the drawer below the plates. Napkins are in the drawer next to the silverware. If you want to grab a couple of glasses I'll get some juice as well."

She selected what she needed, walked to the table, and began setting their places. If it had been light she was sure the view out the sliding glass doors adjacent to the table would be spectacular. As it was she could see the lights of Homer twinkling below and across the bay other faint lights were visible. He came over and placed marmalade, butter and salt and pepper on the table. He returned to the stove, removed the lid and, satisfied that the omelet had set, added the bacon, onions and cheese. He folded the omelet over and covered it again briefly. After a moment he cut it in half and divided it between two plates. He poured two cups of coffee, placed a slice of toast on each plate and carried it all to the table. He retrieved grapefruit juice from the refrigerator and poured them each a glass. They sat down and ate in silence, each absorbed in their own thoughts.

When her plate was embarrassingly clean she sighed contentedly and pushed herself back from the table. "That was absolutely delicious and hit the spot perfectly. The toast was incredible. Is it locally baked?"

"I guess you could say so. It's my own recipe. It's sourdough onion rye and the starter I use is over 25 years old."

"A man of many talents. You don't by any chance do windows too do you?"

He chuckled as he found he really enjoyed her sense of humor.

"I have to keep some of my secrets in reserve. Wouldn't want you to lose interest."

"I can't imagine ever being bored around you. Certainly haven't been since the moment we met."

They carried their dishes to the sink, scraped them and loaded the dishwasher. They filled their coffee cups and stood by the island as if unsure of what to say or do next. He finally broke the silence.

"Let's go out and bring in your things and you can get settled and unpacked. Then maybe we can sit and talk for a bit."

She nodded and they went to the garage. As Meagan led the way back David was pleased to see she went directly to his bedroom without hesitation.

"If you'd like to unpack, there's space in the closet to hang your things. And the bottom drawers in the bureau are empty. I'll wait for you in the living room. Take your time."

As she hung her clothes she found she was relieved to see no sign of another woman in the large walk-in closet. Nor was there when she put her toiletries in the bathroom. She was glad because she wanted their time together to be something special. She didn't want to share what she was feeling. She considered showering but didn't want to remove the remnants of their lovemaking, to wash any part of him off of her. Returning to the bedroom she retrieved the talisman, unwrapped it and placed it on the nightstand beside the bed. She stored the empty suitcases in the closet and headed to the living room.

When she entered she found he had started a fire. Music was playing softly and she recognized the strains of Pachelbel's Canon in D. A plush rug was in front of the fireplace and upon it he had assembled a collection of large pillows. He was reclining against one watching her.

"Good choice of music. Seems to fit the mood."

"It's my all-time favorite song. The first time I drove to Homer I pulled off at the overlook before you get into town and listened to it as I took in the view. It somehow conveyed so much of what I was feeling. As the crescendo built so did my attraction and desire for what I saw in front of me. I use it now not only for sheer enjoyment but to celebrate special times."

She absorbed the meaning of his words. She bent down and gave his cheek a gentle kiss. She found a comfortable seat on the pillows so she was facing him but kept a little distance between them. If they were indeed going to talk she couldn't be too close and touching him or all conversation would be lost. She sat and waited for whatever he wished to discuss.

CHAPTER 20

"I'm a believer in being up front and direct," he began. "I've found if I tell the truth I don't have to remember who I told what to."

She tensed as she wondered what was coming next. She thought what they had shared had been as special for him as it had been for her. Maybe she was wrong about it, maybe he was used to this. She sat waiting for where he would go and what he would say. His next words quelled her doubts and she felt herself relax.

"I've never been with a woman before who makes me feel like I feel with you, who makes me feel so gloriously alive. When we made love all the little self-protection barriers I've spent my life putting up just fell away as if they'd never been there in the first place. It was really disconcerting because I've never allowed myself to be vulnerable like that. It's pretty scary for me."

"I won't hurt you, David."

"I didn't mean to imply you would deliberately hurt me, that's not it at all."

He struggled to put what he was feeling into words.

"I've spent a lot of my life keeping myself from being hurt. Not physically. I've always pushed the envelope physically, that's why I excelled at sports. But emotionally it's been a different story. Its not that I think I'm fragile or anything. But I'm definitely guarded. It's difficult for me to trust anyone enough to allow them in there at the very core of me. But I know I want you in there, Meagan. I truly know I do. I just don't know how to take the barriers down by myself. I've tried before but they keep popping back up. It's as if they have a mind of their own. And just like I said I don't want to be hurt, I don't want to hurt you either."

She thought about how to respond for a moment.

"This is pretty new territory for me, too. Back at the cabin you suggested we just take it a day at a time and see where we end up. When we find where that is I'm sure we'll both know what needs to come next."

She could see the relief in his face. She knew it had been difficult for him to share his feelings with her. She had spent a lot of her life dealing with things on the surface rather than pushing down inside as well. She wasn't quite sure why it seemed okay for her to probe deeper inside now. But it was.

He got to his feet and reached down to help her to hers. He took her hand and led her to the bedroom. They both took their clothes off. He noticed she had placed her talisman beside the bed. As she prepared to remove her pouch he took hold of her hand and stopped her.

"Leave it on for tonight, please. I'd like to have those close to us tonight. I know I said something about a repeat performance but would you mind if I just held you for a while. I think I'm more emotionally spent than I realized. But I really, really want to hold you tonight."

She thought she had never heard a more romantic request in her life. They climbed into bed and he put his arms around her. Little was said. He simply held her against him and she found they fit perfectly together. After a while she turned to face away from him and drifted off to sleep. He continued to hold her as they both slept.

CHAPTER 21

Morning comes early to Homer in May and it was already bright daylight outside when Meagan awoke. She glanced at the clock that indicated it was only 7 am. She was the alone in the bed and she wondered when David had gotten up. She hadn't felt or heard him leave. She took a shower and dressed. When she walked into the kitchen she saw him sitting at the island peering at his laptop screen, a mug of coffee beside him. He looked up as she approached and smiled a good morning.

"What time did you get up?"

"A little before six. I tend to be an early riser. I have this weird thing where if I don't get up and greet the day I feel like I've lost something I can't get back. I've always been like that. It's harder to make sense of it here in Alaska because you could go without sleep in the summer and do nothing but sleep in the winter. But that's how I've always operated. I was tempted to stay but couldn't go back to sleep and didn't want to wake you. You were sleeping so peacefully. Did I disturb you?"

"Nope. I tend to fall into a deep sleep a couple of hours before I wake up. What's with the computer?"

"I was just checking the news to see if the jolt I felt last night had registered on any of the seismic indicators anywhere. Apparently the tremor was confined to this house."

He grinned up at her.

You're good with words, Mr. Solomon. I'll give you that."

"Oh, so we're formal now Miss Turner."

He got up and stood behind her. He put his arms around her waist and nuzzled her neck. She smelled fresh and desirable.

"What can I do to get back to our previous informal status?"

"I don't think you're having a problem figuring that out."

The urge to just pick her up and carry her back to bed, to peel her clothes off and explore her body again, came suddenly. The strength of what he felt was astounding. He released her and stepped back.

"I want you again, Meagan. I can't believe how much I want you again. I just need to tell you that before we get the day underway. There's a ton of things I want to show you and share with you. And we need to figure out all this prophecy stuff. And I know we'll go back to bed again. But I still want you to know the feelings you instill in me."

She turned to face him and kissed him tenderly.

"I feel it as well, David, I truly do." She smiled mischievously. "But if I'm going to be able to see anything of Homer I need a guide. I can't have you collapsed in bed so exhausted you can't get up."

"Is that a challenge?"

"Think of it as a promise. I'm as anxious as you are to get back in bed together. But first I want to see everything that drew you to this place."

They sat side by side at the island. Breakfast consisted of coffee, a bowl of Fiber One with blueberries and a glass of juice. After cleaning up they grabbed windbreakers and prepared to leave. Meagan dashed back into the bedroom and retrieved her camera. They got in his Jeep and drove off.

He wanted to show her the B&B first. They continued further along Diamond Ridge Drive before turning off on a side road. A short ways down the road they passed through a gate with a sign above it announcing their arrival at Kachemak View Bed & Breakfast. He pulled into the enormous garage and parked. They got out and walked the short distance along the walkway to the main building. Inside he introduced her to Carolyn and Jerry Clayton. Carolyn indicated she had some things needing discussion with David and Jerry offered to give her a tour of the facilities.

They were standing in the great room. One long side was comprised of a wall of windows facing the city, bay and mountains beyond. Because of the way the lodge was positioned her view was more panoramic and she could also see across Cook Inlet to the mountains and volcanoes there. It was breathtaking to behold.

The room itself was quite large, Jerry told her it was 30' by 50' with 25' ceilings and a wall on one side held a massive stone fireplace with bookshelves on either side. A number of sofas, love seats, overstuffed chairs, card tables with chairs and desks were placed throughout. Paintings, photographs and knickknacks scattered throughout reflected the Alaskan setting. He said the intent was to create an environment where people could choose to sit alone or in groups depending on their wishes at the moment.

The wall opposite the fireplace held a large open doorway leading to a dining area. He explained how the seating in this room could again be quickly rearranged to allow people to all eat together or in smaller clusters, even alone. The dining room had windows on two sides allowing people to gaze at the majestic scenery while they ate. A door on the back led to a kitchen that seemed as if it would be suited for a large hotel. Jerry proudly showed her through his domain, including the walk-in freezer and refrigerator. A pantry the size of most master bedrooms held gleaming stainless steel shelves and cupboards capable of holding supplies for a small army. The kitchen and storage had its own private access door from the garage so it could be restocked without interfering with guest activities and views.

Adjacent to the kitchen he showed her the laundry and housekeeping facilities. Everything she had seen was state-of-the-art and displayed pride of ownership. David insisted on first class appearance and maintenance in everything he explained, whether it was behind the scenes or in full view of guests. Beyond this was the office area where Carolyn did most of her work. They would go in there later after she and David had concluded their business. His and Carolyn's quarters were located above the kitchen, laundry and office area.

He led her outside to the massive covered front porch dotted with rockers, swings and chairs for sitting and admiring the views. The porch wrapped around to a large deck outside the dining room containing a series of tables for guests who chose to eat outside when the weather permitted.

He walked along a lighted pathway, past an enormous hot tub and smaller building containing a sauna, to the first of the cabins. It was similar in feel to the one she had at the Kenai Princess Lodge although each of these featured a private bedroom in addition to the convertible sofa in the main area. He explained that each of the other cabins was similar with slight variations in the arrangement and interior color schemes to make them feel unique to the guests. Each could accommodate anywhere from one to four guests.

On their way back to the main lodge they passed a large stone fire pit surrounded by benches. This was where they would build campfires in the evening for guests to sit outside and talk, roast marshmallows or simply gaze at the scenery below and the sky above.

Meagan was impressed. From the little she knew of David she had figured he would do things right but this surpassed anything she could have imagined. She said so to Jerry and found he felt the same way.

"I still have to pinch myself occasionally so I know

it's real. I worked in a first class place before at the Alyeska Resort in Girdwood. It's beautiful and done well but it is a big operation. Here we've managed to capture and present all that in a small and private setting. When David originally explained his vision to us we knew we wanted to be part of it. I'll let Carolyn share with you how she feels," he said as they entered the office area.

Carolyn was sitting behind her desk while David sat facing her in one of two chairs. When they entered the room, David rose and explained he needed to run down into town to talk with a couple of the contractors and review some of the finishing touches that needed to be completed before the B&B could begin receiving guests. He said he'd be back in an hour or two and then he'd take her down to Homer and show her the sights. He kissed her lightly on the cheek and departed.

Carolyn and Jerry glanced at each other in surprise. To the best of their recollection David had never acted so casually affectionate with another woman in the year they had known him. Yet here was someone he'd known only a few days and she already seemed to be a part of his life. This would bear a little closer look.

Meagan looked around the office. While the walls and some of the furnishings maintained part of the rustic look and feel, all the equipment was modern and state of the art. Carolyn's desktop was made of a large slab of pine or cedar that had been varnished till it gleamed. Behind her comfortable leather chair a similar surface on the credenza held a monitor, small printer/fax/copier and keyboard. The office was neat and tidy with everything in its place. She felt she and Carolyn would get along just fine because that is how she, too, maintained her workspace. Jerry excused himself as he had a few things that required his attention and exited the room.

Carolyn politely inquired about what Meagan did for a living and was pleasantly surprised to find she was an accountant. "I was a business major myself. Got my MBA at Wharton. Never figured I'd end up in Alaska managing a place like this. But then I never figured I'd end up married to a chef, either. Has its advantages."

Meagan liked her immediately. She wasn't boastful or pretentious but seemed really down to earth. She relayed how she'd been climbing the corporate ladder since graduate school and was now on the brink of a partnership. Carolyn's eyebrow rose as she realized just what Meagan had accomplished to date professionally and asked what brought her to Alaska. She nodded sympathetically when Meagan told her of the death of her father and her mother's inability to come with her on the trip. She told her she'd met David at the Kenai Princess Lodge but didn't go into detail about how that occurred. She said David had invited her down to see what he was doing and she had accepted.

Carolyn asked if she'd like to stay here at the B&B while she looked around Homer. Meagan hesitated for a moment and then said she was staying with David. She looked at Carolyn and hesitated, uncertain about what the reaction would be.

"My God, woman, how did you manage to accomplish that in such a short time? To the best of my knowledge David has never had anyone stay over with him since he's been here. And that's not because no one has tried to snag him. Good heavens but you must really be a pistol." She looked at Meagan with renewed interest.

Meagan blushed. She hadn't shared all the unusual things going on and didn't want to without first talking it over with David but also felt she owed her some explanation. She shrugged it off by replying lightly, "I'll be happy to share my technique but I think it would be better understood after a glass or two of something containing alcohol."

"My goodness, Meagan, if I won't take you up on that. Now ain't this a hoot!"

Silently, Carolyn was reconsidering her plans. She had just finished talking with David about the need to add a financial person to their staff. While she herself was proficient in finances and accounting the reality was the skills she possessed were needed more in building and managing the business. She knew from her lengthy conversations with David that coming up with an idea and transforming it into reality was his forte but that he would quickly lose interest if he had to run it on a day-to-day basis. Could Meagan be that person? Given her background and the level she'd attained, would she even be interested? At the present time they didn't need a full-time person but it would soon grow into that. She thought from her initial impression that she'd enjoy spending time with Meagan but this was a whole new direction. Her mind was whirling and she made a quick decision.

"Have you and David made plans for tonight?"

"I haven't made any. I don't know about him."

"I'll take care of it and clear it with David." She lifted her phone and used the intercom to connect her with Jerry. "Hey, babe," she said into the phone, "there's a change of plans for tonight. I know. I know what we had scheduled. But we're going to entertain the boss and," she looked over at Meagan, "his lady. Make some reservations at 7 at Finn's Pizza and then give John a call at the Salty Dawg and get us a table for four for the show." She looked up at Meagan. "Hobo Jim's in town and he'll be at the Salty Dawg at 9 tonight. It's an Alaskan experience you don't want to miss."

"I'm just along for the ride."

"Now let me show you around and tell you what I do here in our little frontier version of Camelot."

They grabbed some coffee and went outside and sat on the porch. Carolyn told her how they were slowly assembling the pieces to enable each guest to come and create their own unique Alaskan experience. Arrangements had been made for a wide range of activities. Jerry was handling all the dining and catering part of things, the lodging was done and final touches were being added, they were working with travel agents and cruise lines to obtain referrals, she herself was working with a web designer to create a presence that drew people who were making their own plans. There were a lot of varied yet coordinated things in progress. It was all coming together slowly but surely. Still she and David were feeling they had overlooked something. They were missing a piece, but they had been unable to put their finger on it. Never mind, they'd figure it out and deal with it in time.

Meagan conveyed her positive reaction to it all. She was certain it would be a resounding success with all the planning, effort and attention to detail that had been put into it. It was pleasant to sit outside with a view like this actually discussing business. She thought how dramatically different it was from the business environment in which she'd been functioning in San

Diego. She was going to have to start thinking about that again soon because her scheduled time in Alaska was drawing to a close. For now she just needed to focus on being here so what time she did have wasn't contaminated and ruined by association.

They were still sitting on the deck when David returned. Carolyn informed him of the plans for the evening and watched his reaction closely. She thought she saw a flicker of frustration briefly before he enthusiastically embraced the idea. She suspected he'd had other more private plans for him and Meagan and she filed that thought away. Despite the fact she was eight years older than David and that he was her boss she'd always thought of him as the little brother she'd wanted but never had. She cared deeply for him and enjoyed working with him. They had shared a lot of both professional and personal things with each other in the year they had been working together. She knew he was looking for a meaningful relationship even though he didn't always seem to know it himself. She wondered if this might be it.

"So what else is on the agenda today?" she asked him.

"Thought I'd give Meagan a tour of Homer and the area. I'm glad we got a good day for it."

"As long as you're back in time for the pizza. If

you're not there by 7 I'll order for you and you'll have to take what you get."

David winced knowing her predilection for anchovies. While he didn't mind an occasional taste of the salty little fish he didn't like it when their taste and smell permeated throughout his pizza.

"We'll be there beforehand. If you're late you'll have to be content with my selection."

Meagan watched the interaction, envying them their good-natured banter. It was nothing like the stodgy, more formal interactions that took place in her office. Come to think of it, she'd never heard a light conversation take place between any of the partners and her associate peers.

David rose and said they'd best be getting going now. Meagan thanked Carolyn for her company and remarked on the beautiful and special setting she was part of creating. She told her she'd look forward to seeing her this evening and with a wink asked if a glass or two of spirits might be part of the occasion. Carolyn opined that it just might be the case as she stood thoughtfully and watched the two leave. She needed to let Jerry know of her suspicions about these two so he could watch for signs tonight.

CHAPTER 22

David was glad to be leaving the B&B. While he'd wanted Meagan to see what he was creating he realized he wanted to monopolize her time. He didn't want to share her, not even with two people whom he cared deeply about. He was aware their time together was limited if Meagan proceeded with her planned departure and he didn't want to waste a minute of it.

When they were seated in the Jeep he turned toward her and took her in his arms. His mouth found hers and he forgot where he was and what he had been planning to do. All he could think about was how good she tasted and how right it felt to hold her like this. He sighed and concentrated completely on the kiss.

Meagan had been expecting, maybe it was only hoping, he would kiss her. What she hadn't expected, or perhaps conveniently forgotten, is how quickly and passionately she responded to him. Her mind went blank and her body took over. Her arms went around his neck and she focused her efforts on feeling as many of the overwhelming sensations as she could. She moaned softly and sank deeper into oblivion.

She finally had to come up for air. Pulling back she looked at him.

"It's a good thing I already had my seat belt fastened."

"The car's not moving."

"So you say. Feels like it is. Something's moving, that's for sure."

"I just couldn't wait any longer to hold you again and to kiss you."

"You didn't hear me complain did you?"

"Now that you mention it, no, I didn't hear any complaints."

"My mama didn't raise no fools."

God, but he enjoyed her. He liked her humor, her mind, her looks, her body. Yes, he definitely liked her body. But it was the whole package that attracted him. He couldn't seem to get enough. This must be what a moth feels when it is drawn to a flame. He wondered if Meagan would end up burning him. Right now it didn't matter because he hadn't restrained himself. Even if he wanted to hold back, and he didn't want to, he couldn't. Or was it he wouldn't? He wanted her to know everything about him, his strengths, his weaknesses, his needs, his fears, his wants, his desires. He wanted her to know it all. As long as when she did she would still want him. And that was the key to it wasn't it? He could control letting her know the different pieces. He couldn't control her reaction after that. Could he handle the pain if she got to know all there was to him and decided to leave? He knew he could deal with it on an intellectual level. It was in his guts that the pain would be more than he thought he could endure. He started the car and their tour of Homer began.

Meagan watched in fascination as his face reflected the conflicting emotions he processed through. She wanted to reach out to him, to soothe him, to make the pain go away. But she also knew he needed to reach his own conclusions on whatever was causing his internal tug-of-war. She wanted to be there for him when the struggle was over. She was startled to realize that was true.

"So where are we going?" is all she said.

"Do you get seasick easily?"

She thought about it. Even though she was living not far from the water in a San Diego condo she really didn't spend any time out on the water. On the beach, to be sure she went there, but not on the water itself. Still, she used to go out fishing periodically with her father when she lived at home. Of course, those were her teenage years.

"I don't really know. I don't think so. I used to go out fishing with my father but the last time was probably eleven years ago. I didn't get sick then and we were out in some choppy seas. At least they seemed like it to me."

"I thought we could take a boat ride over to Seldovia. It's a small town across the bay from Homer. It would let you see Homer from a different perspective."

"You're the tour guide but it sounds fine to me."

She looked around as he wound his way down from the hills into Homer itself. She saw the hospital, he drove her down the main street pointing out restaurants and shops and stores. Then he headed back and took the road leading out to the Homer Spit.

"We'll be coming out here to meet the Claytons later. Finn's Pizza and the Salty Dawg are just a little past where I'm going to turn off."

He turned left into a parking lot and turned off the Jeep. They walked through a gate he unlocked down to where a bunch of boats were docked.

"Alaskan Adventures keeps its boat here. We'll use it to run fishing trips for halibut and salmon or just to ferry guests to different places like Seldovia. I haven't had it out for a while and it could stand to be run."

They walked along the dock and he stopped beside one of the longer boats in the harbor. Its name identified it as the Sea 'Scape. She laughed quietly at implications of the name. Like everything she'd seen so far connected to David it was immaculate and gleaming. That was a far cry from many of the other boats in the harbor. She liked it that he took the time to maintain things in pristine condition. She decided that it spoke to the quality he wanted to offer to his clientele. And the respect he had for them as well as himself. After climbing on board she walked around with him as he started the motors, worked his way through a pre-launch checklist, and prepared to cast off.

"It's a 38 foot Bay Weld aluminum boat built by a local company called Bay Welding. They build boats designed specifically for the conditions you encounter up here. You have plenty of power with the twin Suzuki 400 horsepower engines. Because it's aluminum it's lighter than most boats of this size so you have better fuel economy and thus a longer range. I had it built last year and it has all the modern gadgetry you'd expect. It's virtually unsinkable but still there's a motorized dinghy on the roof for emergencies or just for exploring. You lower it with that boom over on the port side. That's left side for you landlubbers."

"You drive something this big by yourself?"

"Yes, but of course this time I have a crew member to order around," he said smiling. She liked it when he smiled and the worries fell away from his face. She resolved to do everything she could to make that happen as often as possible.

"Aye, aye captain. Just tell me what to do."

David went up to the bridge and checked all the gauges. Things were warmed up and all the needles read as they should. He instructed her to release the bow line and then the one on the stern. Soon they were underway and moving at a sedate pace out of the harbor. Meagan went up to the bridge and joined him.

When they had cleared the harbor and were out in the open bay he increased the speed. The wind picked up and Meagan found her hair streaming behind her as she gazed out. It felt good to be out here. She liked the smell of the ocean and the feel of the wind on her face. It's good to be alive and doing this she thought. She sat back in the seat and enjoyed the ride.

They were approaching a larger island with a smaller one adjacent to it. He suggested she get her camera ready so she retrieved it from her daypack. When they reached Gull Island there were thousands of seagulls on it. It looked like the rocky surface had been painted in seagulls. The smell of it was powerful but not really offensive. She took a number of shots including some close-ups of individual gulls.

Soon they were back up to cruising speed as they continued west in the bay. Before long he was turning into what he informed her was Seldovia Bay and soon the town of Seldovia appeared. He pulled in the harbor and expertly maneuvered the boat to a spot in the visitor's docking area. They secured the boat and set off to explore on foot.

He asked if she was hungry and she said she could handle something. He steered them to the Madfish Restaurant just across from the harbormaster's office. They shared an order of halibut and chips. They each had a beer. After lunch they resumed their walk.

The town itself was small and compact and everything was within walking distance of the harbor. They ventured into shops and just poked around and enjoyed the afternoon, the sights and being with each other. She thought he was remarkably easy to be with. He wasn't demanding or demeaning. He seemed genuinely interested in her and what she had to say. He appreciated it when she became excited about something that caught her eye and wanted to capture a moment in time with a picture. After determining the things that interested her he took the time to point them out so she might enjoy them. He seemed more relaxed now than he had when he had returned to the B&B. This definitely was a day for creating memories. Come to think of it most every day since she had stepped foot on the Coral Princess had been a day for memories. What funny twists and turns her life had taken of late. One day she had been getting on a plane in San Diego and now only nine days later she was in a remote little town in Alaska that felt like it was a million miles from anywhere. And she was in the company of a wonderful man who had brought her body to life last night. He had played her like a virtuoso plays a piano. And the music produced was superb. She was looking forward to a repeat performance. She smiled at the thought and took his hand in hers as they walked.

David, too, was enjoying himself immensely. He couldn't remember the last time he had just taken off and done something relaxing. He knew he wouldn't have done it had it not been for Meagan appearing and wanting to know about Homer. And him. She wanted to know about him. She was so much fun to be with. She was interested in so many things. And her enthusiasm when she became interested was contagious. It made him want to share things with her just to see her unfettered reaction. He admired her courage. When he had invited her to change her plans and come be with him she had only briefly hesitated before agreeing. That had taken a lot of moxie and he admired her for it.

And wasn't it incredible that Carolyn had cornered him this morning and put forth her rationale for needing to hire a fiscal staff member. That was playing right into Meagan's strong suit. Just like all the coincidences Meagan had encountered with her dreams and talisman and all, it was just too serendipitous to be random chance. Was someone or something scripting all this out? All he could surmise is there were factors at work beyond his understanding. He had no idea if she might be willing to throw all the time she'd invested in her accounting career away to move to Alaska for a shot at a job that not only would certainly pay less than she currently made but really didn't offer any career path either. It was only going to be a half-time position to start. Whether the business would pan out or not only added to the uncertainty. And then there was the issue of whether or not the relationship would pan out. Both of their track records left something to be desired. People in the financial field tended not to be spontaneous risk takers. But she had come to Homer with him, hadn't she? Was he being too selfish by trying to stack the deck in his favor so she would choose to be here with him? What was he willing to offer to get that choice to become a reality?

They returned to the boat and set out on the voyage back to Homer. The seas were relatively calm and they made good time without incident. It was a pleasant trip and they were both relaxed when they arrived. After securing the boat they climbed in the Jeep for the short jaunt to the restaurant.

CHAPTER 23

Carolyn and Jerry were just entering Finn's when David and Meagan pulled up in front. They were quickly seated and perused the menu. Meagan commented on the eclectic mix of pizzas from which to choose. They ordered the Spring and Summer Special (seared zucchini, roasted red peppers, crimini mushrooms on a three cheese pizza with organic red sauce) and a Blue Pear (garlic and olive oil sauce, gorgonzola, fresh mozzarella, pears and pine nuts) and agreed to all share. They ordered a pitcher of Homer Brewing Company's Broken Birch Bitter and headed upstairs to the solarium where they found a corner table with an amazing view of the bay and surroundings. They settled in, raised their glasses in a silent toast, and the conversation started to flow.

Meagan learned that Carolyn and Jerry had met

while she was obtaining her MBA at Wharton in Philadelphia. He had attended the New Orleans School of Cooking and come to the Culinary Institute of the USA in Philadelphia for additional training. They met at a bar in the downtown area and had known they wanted to be together from the start. After graduation they had looked for locations where they could both work in the fields they had each chosen and had spent time in Phoenix, Portland Oregon, and then had been recruited by the Alyeska Resort in Girdwood. That is where they had met David.

Originally they had both wanted children but for whatever reasons that had not happened. Carolyn felt it was because she had undergone radiation treatment for a thyroid problem while she was a baby that resulted in her whole little body being exposed. Her family had been living in Panama and that was the way they treated such conditions at the time. That type of treatment was no longer used but the damage had been done. But she and Jerry had adapted to the reality and moved on with their lives. They both loved Alaskan life.

After refilling Meagan's glass Carolyn noted this was her second beer and asked how she had met David. The two had discussed how to share their situation with the Claytons during their boat ride back from Seldovia. They had decided to be as upfront as possible no matter the reaction. Their pizzas arrived and while everyone dug in Meagan gave a brief overview of all that had happened since she got on the Coral Princess. She omitted the details of their lovemaking but the rest was left intact.

Not blinking an eye, Carolyn asked if David kissed as good as she thought he would.

"Trust me, he's very accomplished at the art of kissing."

"All he's ever given me is a couple of quick pecks on the cheek. Must be an age thing."

David decided discretion was the better part of valor and did not participate in the evaluation of his kissing skills. Instead he turned to Jerry and asked what he thought of Meagan's tale. Jerry said that he, like David, didn't simply dismiss things out of hand if he couldn't explain them. When he'd been in New Orleans he had been exposed to a culture in which mysticism and voodoo was simply taken for granted as part of everyday life. He thought most of the legends and superstitions probably had a basis in reality although the true meaning and events might have become obscured as it was passed down numerous times. He likened it to the game of telephone in which someone starts a story and it is passed from one person to another until by the time it reaches the final person it is markedly different from the story that began. Each telling simply incorporated the flavor and experiences of all the people who participated. At its conclusion you could find vestiges of the original tale but it had taken on a life of its own.

Ever since the group had first sat down and begun to talk Carolyn had continued to silently observe Meagan and David to watch how they interacted. She liked what she saw. They both were affectionate and displayed it by absently reaching over and touching each other. They obviously cared about each other a great deal. Each also had a healthy respect for the other individual. They seemed comfortable together. And suited. As the group was preparing to leave for the Salty Dawg she made her decision and turned to Meagan.

"Is it possible for you to swing by the B&B tomorrow morning about 11 am? I have something I'd like to discuss with you."

"I suppose so," Meagan said glancing at David to see if there was any conflict. Seeing none she indicated she would be there at the appointed time.

As they walked the short distance to the Salty Dawg Saloon David shared with her a little of its history as it had transitioned from an 1897 cabin to Homer's first post office, a railroad station, and a coal mining office over a period of twenty years. In 1909 it had received an addition and became a schoolhouse, post office again and then a grocery store. In the 1940's it became an office for Standard Oil Company. It continued to grow in size during the 1950's and in April of 1957 it became the Salty Dawg Saloon. The Alaska Territory became the 49th state in April of 1959. After the "Good Friday" earthquake of March 1964 it was moved to its present location. The distinctive lighthouse tower was added to cover a water storage tank. It was now considered one of Homer's more distinctive landmarks. He said it now was owned and operated by John Warren. Meagan was intrigued with the rustic exterior appearance.

When they entered she was amazed. It was dark and noisy but the thing you couldn't miss were all the signed dollar bills decorating the ceiling and walls. There were thousands and thousands of them everywhere. Randomly interspersed were some bras and other unidentifiable objects. She was introduced to John Warren and they were shown to the table that had been held for them. It was obvious they were regulars and well liked. Four bottles of Alaskan Amber were brought to their table and David told her they had nothing on tap here. She looked around the room, enjoying the smoky, dark and noisy atmosphere. There were dirty fishermen with crusted blood still on their hands sitting next to what were obviously tourists. It was difficult to talk over the din that filled the room. David leaned close to her ear and said it would quiet down when Hobo Jim began to perform. He said it was about the only time he knew of that the patrons would shut up.

Hobo Jim entered and made a round of the tables, greeting a number of the regulars by name. When he came to their table he was introduced to Meagan and welcomed her to Alaska. She didn't know what she had expected but it wasn't this. He didn't look like her idea of a hobo, he looked more like a cowboy, maybe even a younger version of Willie Nelson. David explained he had been a fisherman, logger, even a cowboy before finally turning to writing songs about his occupations and his wilderness lifestyle. In 1994 the state legislature and governor had proclaimed Hobo Jim to be "Alaska's State Balladeer." He was now an Alaskan legend and had recently returned from entertaining the troops in Afghanistan.

When he took the stage the crowd did indeed become quieter. They listened intently as Hobo Jim sang songs that were both humorous and melancholy. She learned of life in remote locations and the hardships of difficult physical work in the seas and bush around them. She was entranced by the visions he created in her mind as he sang of the Alaska he knew and loved. She joined with the crowd as they belted out the lyrics of "I did. I did. I did the Iditarod Trail." She did indeed feel like she had been shown a side of Alaska that few got to see.

As they walked back to their cars Jerry looked up at the sky and informed them the weather was changing, that they probably wouldn't see the sun tomorrow. They got in David's car and made their way back to his house. She found herself somewhat saddened that the evening was coming to a close although she was looking forward to being alone again with David. She was quiet as they drove and when they entered the house.

CHAPTER 24

"Is everything okay?" he asked.

"Yeah, it's fine. I was just thinking about all the feelings I have about Alaska as I listened to his songs tonight. He really has a knack for making it come to life."

"That he does. It's a special place for him as it is for many of us who live here."

As they stood in the living room in front of the fireplace she took his face in her hands and looked him in the eyes.

"You're just as special as Alaska is. I don't think I told you how extraordinary last night was for me. And I don't just mean the sex although I've never before felt so fulfilled, so full of life and emotion. What I'm talking about is the complete intimacy I felt when you simply held me. It was as if nothing in the world but us existed. I've never experienced anything like that before and I realized it's something that was missing in previous relationships. Thank you for giving me that."

"I received back every bit as much as I gave, maybe more. I don't think I've ever fallen asleep so peacefully."

She pulled his face to hers and kissed him softly and tenderly. Pulling back she smiled.

"Don't think you're off the hook for tonight, though, Mister. I want more. A lot more."

They held hands and walked towards the bedroom. As she was sitting on the bed removing her shoes and socks she asked what he thought Carolyn wanted to talk about with her. He said he thought he knew but wasn't positive. They'd find out when it happened. He didn't want to tell her he was certain Carolyn would offer her a job. He was afraid she wouldn't accept it. And he wanted her to take it. A part of him was also afraid she would accept and what that would mean for him.

She unclasped her pouch and placed it on the nightstand beside the talisman. She wondered what tomorrow would bring. For the moment she decided to focus on what would be tonight. When they climbed into bed she turned to face him.

"Let me give to you tonight, David. I have so many feelings about you bottled up inside me that I feel like I'm going to explode. This seems to be the best way I can let them out. I need to do this. For both of us."

She put her fingers to his lips when he started to reply, silencing him. "Shhh," she said. "Don't say anything for a while. Just lie there and take what I have to give."

In her previous experiences she had never taken the lead in sex. She thought she knew what men enjoyed and wanted and wasn't shy. But she had always reacted to their lead and their indication. She became aware of the power she held as she initiated the activity.

She began by just stroking him gently. She rubbed his face, his neck, his shoulders, his chest and his arms. She massaged his hands and each individual finger. She kept her touch soft and tender. She wanted him to feel safe with her touch and with her. She moved down and stroked his stomach before reaching his legs. She worked all the way down to his feet and massaged each toe. She had him turn over and she repeated the process back up his body before arriving at his head. She rubbed his thick head of hair, her fingers working his scalp.

When he was finally relaxed she turned him back over and repeated the process with her lips. She took her time and nipped and sucked gently on him as she caressed his body with kisses. She heard his sighs and soft moans as she proceeded lower. She could tell he was ready as she took him in her mouth to help him along. He reached for her and she pushed his arms back down to the bed.

"Just lie still and feel for the moment, David. I still have more to explore."

She continued to move downward, kissing his legs and feet. She slowly moved back up his body and licked him hungrily. She straddled him and found she was every bit as ready as he was. She heard him murmur her name. She placed his hands on her breasts as she began to ride him. She rode harder, forcing him deeper inside her. He was breathing heavily now and she could tell he was near his peak. His body lifted as he struggled to both hold back and plunge further. His hands tightened around her breasts as he convulsed and filled her. Her own spasms overtook her as she gazed down at him. When they subsided she collapsed to his chest and held him.

He was tempted to just drift off into sleep. His body was completely and utterly sated. He felt as if his bones had dissolved leaving behind a gelatinous mass. He felt good. He felt relaxed. He felt whole.

Meagan moved against him and he lifted his head.

"Do you think we could bottle that and sell it at the B&B? That would certainly be the high point of any guest's Alaskan experience!"

"It is certainly up there on mine."

She nuzzled his chest and clutched him tighter. She wasn't ready to move from this spot just quite yet. She took in his smell and that of their lovemaking. That's what it had been, she understood, it hadn't been simply sex. They had been making love to each other. She suddenly realized she was falling in love with him. She paused while the concept sunk in. The attraction had begun the moment their eyes met. The feelings of love had begun when he attentively listened to her tale, refusing to pass judgment, and then had sat there and held her understanding her need for comfort. And it had continued to grow with everything she came to know about him and share with him. The passion and excitement they shared when making love was an added bonus. Should she share this knowledge with him now? He had demons to exorcise before he would be ready and willing to love. No, she wouldn't add to his burdens at this point. She was content with the knowledge she did indeed love him. But soon it was bound to come out. No way could she keep this bottled up to herself.

CHAPTER 25

Morning arrived all too soon. The day was foggy and overcast, producing a mystical effect as you looked down the hill towards Homer. There were clouds above and a fog bank below creating the feeling you were trapped between cloud layers. Breakfast consisted of a slice of David's toast, berry preserves, coffee and juice. David drove her to the B&B and dropped her off a few minutes before eleven. He said he had a couple of things to do and would be back in a while. He gave her his cell number in case she needed to reach him for anything.

She knocked and entered Carolyn's office at her urging. They hugged and Carolyn held her at length and looked at her. She motioned to a chair and they both sat down. Instead of sitting across from her Carolyn had taken the chair next to her. She turned and took Meagan's hands in hers.

"You're in love with him, aren't you?"

"Does it show that much? I haven't said anything to David about it. He's told me a bit about his mother and his relationship issues and the last thing he needs is to feel pushed or trapped or threatened. But yes, I do love him. I became sure of it last night. I don't know how and why it happened so quickly but it definitely happened."

"It shows if you know what to look for. And I was. I thought it was so last night as I watched the two of you together. At times it was if Jerry and I weren't even on the same planet. You touched each other as if it was the most natural thing in the world to do. When you smiled at one another the room brightened considerably. I recognized what was going on but then I must say I was watching for it."

"Oh, Carolyn, I do love David so. The feelings I have literally take my breath away. This is all so new for me and there's so many other things going on as well. Do you think he knows?"

"In my experience men are generally the last to know about such things. I can tell he's taken with you. But I doubt if he's dug around under the surface to realize what he really feels. I will tell you that I'm happy for him and for you. I liked you from the moment we were introduced and find I'm liking you more each time I see you."

Carolyn arose and went over and hugged Meagan. Then she walked over to her desk chair and sat in it looking across the desk.

"I'm putting my business hat on now and I don't know if what we just talked about is going to make what I have to say any easier or harder for you to consider. I guess we'll see."

Carolyn proceeded to offer Meagan a position as financial manager of Alaskan Adventures. She said it would be a halftime position at first but would evolve into a fulltime position in the very near future. She named a salary that was significantly less than what she currently made. She said the benefits were good and that it was a relatively stress free environment. They all worked together as a team. Any suggestions or opinions Meagan had about any aspect of the operation, financial or otherwise, would be considered and evaluated. She said if Meagan accepted the position she was welcome to stay in one of the guest cabins while she found her own place and got settled. Or that might be a moot point given her relationship with David. She could start when she was ready but she definitely wanted to have someone on board and functioning within a few weeks if possible.

Meagan sat and contemplated the offer. She hadn't been expecting this. It caught her somewhat off guard.

"I'm flattered by your offer. Does David know you are doing this?" She suddenly thought, "Did he have anything to do with this?"

"To answer your questions, no and no. We are very clear that I run the business and make personnel decisions. He does know I'm looking to hire someone for the position. Ironically, that's what I was running by him yesterday when the two of you came. At the time I didn't know of your accounting and financial background. The idea occurred to me when we talked and you shared some of what led up to your trip up here. It seemed you were looking for a change and I thought this might be it."

Meagan was relieved it hadn't been David's idea, that he might have been trying to manipulate her into staying. She hadn't thought that was true and was glad to hear it confirmed. She told Carolyn she'd give careful consideration to the offer and would let her know tomorrow. She was told to take her time and that she hoped things would allow them the opportunity to work together.

She exchanged a few pleasantries with Jerry, got a cup of coffee from the kitchen, and sat in the main room of the lodge. She was lost in thought. She suddenly retrieved her cell phone and dialed a number.

When she was put through to Diane's voicemail she realized she was probably in trial at the moment. She left a brief message telling her she had met the man from her dream and was down in Homer with him. She'd give her a call later when she was off work. She dialed another number.

"Hi, Mom. How are you? How did the surgery go? Is everything fine?"

Helen assured her all was well. The surgery had proceeded as planned and she was receiving hyperbaric treatment at UCLA. The doctors had said the ulcers on her foot were made worse by her diabetes and the intense oxygen therapy should enable the wounds to heal rapidly and completely. After catching her up a bit on the surface details of her trip to date Meagan got to the point of her call.

"Mom, how did you know when you were in love with Dad? Did it just happen all of a sudden?"

Helen considered the question. Now this was a surprise tack for Meagan to take. She hadn't mentioned a man in over a year since her breakup with Richard. Taking a deep breath she forged ahead with her reply.

"Honey, I just knew. I knew it by how I felt when I looked at him, when he touched me, when he spoke to me. I knew it by how it made me feel to touch him, to just be with him. I realized I didn't want to be without him, that he made something feel complete in me that had been missing. Fortunately he felt the same way. Now what brought this on?"

"Mom, I met a man. His name is David and he's special, really something special. He brought a part of me to life that I didn't even know existed. I have all these feelings and emotions just running around throughout me. My brain doesn't want to work when we hold each other."

"Does he live in California?"

"He used to. But now he lives in Homer, Alaska. That's where I am now. Oh, Mom, for the first time in my life I know I'm in love."

Helen thought quickly. Now was not the time to worry about what her daughter was doing. She needed her reassurance and support. "Then he's a very lucky man. Any man would be lucky to have your love. You have so much of it in you to share."

"Thanks. And thanks for being so understanding. I'm still in a daze by all this."

"So what are you going to do?"

"Amazingly enough I've been offered a job here. I'm seriously considering taking it and making a move up here. Actually, I think I've just made that decision. I'm going to move to Alaska! Mom! I'm going to move to Alaska! I'll call you back later. I need to let David know what I'm going to do. Thanks, Mom. I love you."

After the call had been disconnected Helen sat back and thought about it. She hadn't heard such excitement and energy in Meagan's voice since she got accepted to UCLA. She'd gradually lost her spark and enthusiasm as she had struggled to build a career. But now, now all that intensity and enthusiasm was back again. She hoped this David knew what he was getting himself into. She was a powerful woman and needed an equally powerful partner.

CHAPTER 26

David had no idea what awaited him. When he pulled into the garage of the B&B Meagan came over and got in the Jeep before he could shut the motor off. She leaned over and gave him a quick peck on his cheek. Her cheeks were flushed and she was smiling.

"Take me up to the overlook please, David. I know the day is a little dreary but it seems bright to me. I have something to share with you and I'd like to do it there. I hope you don't mind."

Smiling back he put the car in gear and backed out of the garage. He drove down to the Seward Highway and followed it until they arrived at the overlook. He pulled into a spot that looked out over the water. He turned to her waiting.

"Turn on the stereo. Put Pachelbel on for me,

please. Oh God, I'm so excited."

David turned the stereo on and inserted the CD. The music started softly and began building.

"Carolyn offered me a position as financial manager. It is only going to be part time at first but it will evolve into full time soon. I'm going to take it. I'm going to move to Homer. Oh David, I'm so excited. I'm so happy."

He hadn't said a word. He looked stunned. Her voice fell as she continued, "That is unless you don't want me to." She looked down.

"Don't want you to? There is nothing I want more. I was afraid to let myself hope you would want to stay. I didn't want to be disappointed if you didn't. This is incredible news. Let's do something to celebrate!"

He took her in his arms and kissed her. It started out tender but grew in intensity as the import of what she said sank in. His mind couldn't process any more and he concentrated instead on the kiss and holding her. This was what he wanted, what he needed. No correct that, she was what he wanted and what he needed.

"So what would you like to do to celebrate? We can go up to the Alyeska Lodge in Girdwood. They have a great restaurant there. It's only about a three hour drive from here. Or we could go back to the Eagle's Crest Restaurant at the Kenai Princess Lodge. That seems somewhat appropriate. Or there's a place I know in the town of Kenai on the river."

"I think I'd rather just pick up a bottle of wine and go home and be with you. Perhaps we can throw some salmon on the grill or something light. I'd like to sit by the fire with a glass of wine and share the time quietly with you."

"Your wish is my command."

He put the car in gear. They drove down into Homer to The Grog Shop and picked up a couple of bottles of Conundrum. They then drove out to Coal Point Seafood on the spit and picked up some silver salmon fillets. Five minutes later they were back at the house. They walked into the kitchen where he opened one of the wine bottles and filled two glasses. He put the remaining bottle of wine and the salmon in the refrigerator. They adjourned to the living room and he started a fire. He turned the stereo on and soft music soon filled the air.

"I didn't even ask you if you'd like me to move in with you or if you'd rather I get my own place. I guess I shouldn't assume anything."

He wondered what made the doubts appear in her eyes and her voice. He put his fingers under her chin and watched her carefully as he lifted it so she looked at him.

"I don't think I've ever wanted anything more in my life than to have you here with me, Meagan. I think when I bought this home it was with the idea that someday you would appear in my life to share it with me. And now here you are. Now here we are."

They raised their glasses and clicked them together in a toast, then took a sip of the wine. They sat together quietly, lost in their individual thoughts as they contemplated this new wrinkle.

Meagan mentally prepared a checklist. She needed to call Diane later since she'd left a voicemail. Tomorrow she would let Carolyn know. She needed to change her reservation and schedule some time to return to San Diego. She would resign her job and list her condo for sale. She'd put some things in storage and ship the rest to Homer. She asked David if he could leave for a few days to accompany her while she did all this. He said to give him a day or two and he'd do it.

They finished their wine and he fixed dinner. They had grilled salmon, rice, green beans and more wine. They were relaxed and comfortable together. Meagan tried to reach Diane and left another voicemail saying she'd call tomorrow. They went to bed early and their lovemaking was tender and sweet. She fell asleep as he held her.

CHAPTER 27

The next morning she called Carolyn and told her she would accept the position. She would be prepared to start in a week or so. She would first be returning to San Diego for a few days to wrap up some details and prepare for the move. Carolyn was overjoyed at the news, said she was so very much looking forward not only to working together but to getting to know each other better as well. She considered that part a bonus.

David had said he would be able to leave in three days so she logged on to the web and began searching for flights. The best connections left Anchorage early in the morning and got them to San Diego by mid-afternoon. She booked those and scheduled them to return four days later. David had said he'd drive them up to Anchorage the night before and they'd spend the night at the airport. That way he'd have his car to bring anything she shipped back with them. She called McClary & Burns and spoke with the secretary of the VP to whom she reported. She scheduled an appointment with him for 9 am the day after they arrived in San Diego. She called the realtor from whom she had purchased her condo and scheduled time with her for later the same afternoon. She called her Mom and made arrangements for dinner the same evening.

She finally reached Diane and brought her up to date on everything that had transpired since they had separated in Whittier. It took some time to explain and Diane was shocked and not a little envious. She said she'd check her schedule and see if she could possibly get down to San Diego while they were there.

The next three days passed quickly and they soon found themselves en route to San Diego. When their plane landed they took a cab to Meagan's condo. It was a 2 bedroom 2 bath unit located on the ninth floor of a complex on 7th street. It was near the Gaslamp District and overlooked the baseball stadium. It was convenient to her work and much of the downtown nightlife. David thought it looked like a model home and didn't reflect much of the personality of its owner. She told him she'd bought it as an investment and hadn't wanted to do anything that would negatively impact that so she'd basically tried to maintain it as it had looked. It seemed at odds with the Meagan he had come to know in Alaska but he refrained from commenting.   He could tell she was anxious and attributed it to her pending visit to her employer.

The next morning they took a taxi to the office of McClary & Burns. An elevator took them to the 12th floor that was fully occupied by the firm.   David selected a magazine from the rack in the waiting room and said he'd wait there for her while she completed her business.   Meagan had dressed for the occasion in a tailored business suit. She left him and headed into the maze of cubicles and offices.   She went into her managing partner's office. He was on the phone but motioned her to a chair. She sat while he finished his conversation. He began by saying how glad he was that she was back and that there was a lot of work requiring her attention. He didn't even inquire as to how her trip had gone. She told him she'd had a lot of time to think during her time off and had come to tender her resignation, effective immediately.

"I know you've had a tough time of late, Meagan, what with your father's death and your mother's health. But don't you think you're being a bit hasty reacting like this? You know you're on track to become a partner by the end of our fiscal year. Are you sure you've taken all this into consideration? This firm has invested a lot in you and to throw it away like this isn't like the little woman I've watched move her way up the ladder. Perhaps you need to take some more personal time off and think this through a little more."

He leaned back as if confident Meagan would come to her senses and heed his solid fatherly advice. She thought to herself that if she had harbored any doubts about the decision she had made that he had effectively removed them. She couldn't understand how she came to be seduced by the need to prove she could play the game and become a partner. And that was what it was after all, a game. And not one she would ever care to play again.

"I don't need any additional time. My decision is final." She handed him an envelope. "This contains my letter of resignation. I'll clear out my desk and be gone shortly. I'll leave my keys and parking pass with your secretary. You can have my final paycheck deposited electronically to my account. Thank you for your time."

She rose and exited the office before he could formulate a reply. She had not been looking forward to this encounter and was relieved it was over. On the way to her cubicle she stopped by the mailroom and picked up a couple of boxes. She quickly packed her personal belongings and got another associate to help her carry them to the reception area. She dropped her keys and parking pass by the secretary on the way.

David rose to greet her as she came into the room. Without a word he took the box carried by the associate and they quickly left. When they reached the street he hailed a taxi, placed the boxes in the trunk, and got in the back seat. She gave the driver the address of her condo and they were underway.

"So how did it go?" He prodded gently, sensing she needed to talk.

"Better than I expected it would. You know he actually made it easy with his condescending manner. He treated me like I didn't know what I'm doing and need to come to my senses. He actually called me a little woman and had the gall to suggest I might want to take some more personal time and reconsider."

"Sounds like you're angry."

"You're damned right I am. That overbearing supercilious bastard! To think I spent all that time working at that place thinking I was doing the right thing. They really don't care about me as an individual at all. They don't care about anyone as a person."

"That's what I found out about corporate America, too. When I finally couldn't take it any longer I couldn't believe I'd stuck it out as long as I did."

He reached over and took her hand. She leaned against him as she said, "My Dad always told me never to burn my bridges. I didn't heed his advice today. I don't think there's anything left of that one."

They reached her condo and carried the boxes

inside. She sat them on the floor in the living room. She looked at her watch and noticed the realtor would be there in just over an hour. They walked out on the balcony and sat quietly in the sunlight absorbing the view.

The realtor was right on time and Meagan opened the door. She came inside, was introduced to David, and set her briefcase on the coffee table. Removing a stack of papers she handed them to Meagan.

"After you called I took the liberty of drawing up the documents we'd need. All we have to do is fill in the number you want to list it for. Attached to the listing agreement are comps on other units similar to yours that have sold in the past few months. You'll notice they range from a low of $450,000 to a high of $589,000. The low one was a short sale so it skews things a bit. There are two other units for sale in this very complex. One is listed at $579,000 and the other at $585,000. If you want to move yours as quickly as you said you did I'd recommend pricing it as close to $550,000 as you're comfortable with." She looked around and continued. "Given the condition of your unit I'd think you would have a substantial offer in hand in less than thirty days. You bought it for $355,000 and still owe around $250,000 on your mortgage so even after commission and closing costs you'll come out pretty well. This is still a highly desirable neighborhood for the corporate climbers and a lot of MBA graduates are accepting offers this time of year and looking for their new place as their careers take off."

Meagan agreed to list her condo for $549,900, the documents were signed, and the realtor left. In addition to inserting the price in the agreement she had changed the forwarding address to David's place in Homer.

CHAPTER 28

They took Meagan's car. They were scheduled to be at her Mom's at 6 pm. The house in which she had been raised was located in the city of Carlsbad, about 40 miles north of her condo in San Diego. They left shortly before 5 pm to allow for any rush hour traffic.

While not on the ocean, the house did have a distant ocean view from its location on a hillside. The neighborhood was one of solid middle class homes. The houses and grounds of all of them were well maintained. David thought it must have been a pleasant place to grow up.

Meagan threw herself into her Mom's arms when the door opened. After a moment of hugs and kisses she pulled back.

"Mom, this is David Solomon. David, my Mom

Helen Turner."

"Pleased to meet you Mr. Solomon."

"It's David, please." He took Helen's hand in his, cocking his head as he looked at her. "Now I know where Meagan gets her smile. Her whole face lights up when she smiles, just as yours does. It's a wonderful sight to see."

"I see now why Meagan likes being with you, David. Saying sweet things like that to a woman goes a long way."

"It's easy to say them when they're true."

Helen turned and led them into the living room. David looked around with appreciation. It was a warm and comfortable room. There was a fireplace on one end that had held a lot of fires in its time. A picture window across from the sofa looked out to the distant ocean. People had enjoyed life in here. It wasn't new and modern and cold. This was more like a favorite sweatshirt. It just felt good here. He said as much to Helen.

"I never thought when we bought this house that I'd live here for over 30 years. I was pregnant with Meagan and this was going to be our starter home. Now I guess it is our finishing home as well. A lot of memories have been created here." She looked around wistfully, then turned to the two of them sitting together and continued, "It appears we're starting a new set of memories now."

David reached for Meagan's hand and responded to Helen, "We are. I can only hope they are as happy and long lasting as the ones you've made here."

They talked amiably. David told her about Homer and how he loved living there. He shared his dream for Alaskan Adventures. He said after their initial rush with opening the B&B things would start to slow down around September. He would be grateful if she would come to visit as his guest. Helen said she'd enjoy that a great deal as long he invited her while there was still sunlight. He laughed and said that would be the case.

Meagan had made dinner reservations for 7 pm at Vigilucci's Seafood & Steakhouse which sat directly across from the ocean on Carlsbad Highway. She said it had been a place her Dad and Mom went for special occasions and she wanted this to be one for all of them. From their table they watched the colors of the sunset fade across the Pacific Ocean. It was mesmerizing and they watched in awe. The seafood was fresh and prepared well.

After dinner they returned to Helen's for coffee. When Meagan went to the restroom Helen turned to David. "I don't recall seeing Meagan this happy in a long, long time. I appreciate you making that happen for her again. She's a wonderful woman and she deserves to be happy. You realize, of course, she's totally smitten with you."

"I do know that, and the feeling is mutual. I consider myself a very lucky man to have her in my life. She brought light to a part of me that felt pretty dark before her."

Helen watched his face as he spoke. He was definitely sincere about what he said. He cared deeply for Meagan, she could see that in the way he looked at her, how he treated her, even how he casually reached out and touched her from time to time. The fears she had felt when Meagan had told her of the decision to move to Homer eased a bit. She no longer worried about where Meagan was going and the person with whom she would be.

"She won't like my saying this, but please watch over her and take care of her for me. She is going through a lot of change right now and it won't always be upbeat and easy for her. She needs some help."

David crossed the room and took Helen's hands in his. He looked her in the eyes and saw the tears just beneath the surface. He knew it was difficult for her to make such a request.

"You have my word on that. I'll do anything I can

to help her through whatever may come. I have a feeling we'll both be helping each other along the way."

"I was terribly apprehensive when Meagan called and told me she'd only known you a few days and was going to move to Alaska to be with you and work with you. I can see now I didn't need to worry. Thank you for that. And thank you for coming over here to set a mother's fears to rest."

"You're more than welcome. You've raised a wonderful daughter. I'm glad I came not only because I was able to meet you but so I could see yet another side of her. She's a complex person with many facets and I think we've just seen the surface so far. I can't wait to see the rest."

Meagan reentered the room and glanced at the two of them. She gathered up her things and gave her Mom a hug and kiss. They promised to keep in touch more often going forward.

The return trip to San Diego was shorter as the freeway was less crowded. They parked in the underground garage and took the elevator to the 9th floor. Inside Meagan walked through all the rooms deciding which things she'd bring with her and what needed to be stored.

Diane had called and was not going to be able to make it down to meet them. The trials she was involved with were still dragging on and she needed to prepare for the following day. They agreed to talk again the following week.

David had tried to contact his sister in Ventura and had received no response from the voicemail he left. He didn't know whether or not she might be out of town.

The next day was spent packing Meagan's belongings. Two large boxes were taken to UPS and shipped to David's house. Three suitcases contained most of her clothes. Those would go as checked baggage. Several more boxes were transported to her Mom's place. Helen had insisted the garage had plenty of room and there was no need to rent a locker. Meagan was selling the place furnished and if the new owners didn't want the furniture she had made arrangements for it to be consigned at a local secondhand store. They took Meagan's car to a local CarMax office and sold it to them. They returned to the condo in a taxi.

With everything that needed doing completed, they decided to change their tickets and return the next day. Both were anxious to get back to Homer and start the next phase of their lives.

CHAPTER 29

The flight to Anchorage was uneventful. Luggage was retrieved and loaded in David's car. It was a long day and when they reached Homer they stopped for a quick bite to eat before heading up to the house. They left Meagan's belongings in the car to deal with the next day.

Meagan called Carolyn in the morning and told her she'd be in the following morning to begin her new position. David was off taking care of a number of things he'd put on hold during their trip and she was left to put her things away. She had never lived with anyone before and it felt strange to try and create her own space in someone else's house. David had done his best to make the transition easy, moving some of his less used clothes into a guest bedroom closet and freeing up more drawer space in the bureau in their bedroom. As she unpacked she reflected on the time since the two had connected.

The first couple of times they had made love were incredible. She had never known her body was capable of such intense and pleasurable feelings. And she had experienced them both when he gave to her and she gave to him. They had made love since then several times and each time had been both gentle and exciting as they became acquainted with each other's desires and preferences. What she found most fulfilling were the times they simply held each other in silence. She felt content and peaceful in his arms, as if all her worries and cares were held at bay and she was safe and secure.

Out of bed he treated her with respect and consideration, genuinely interested in her opinions and wishes. He had sincerely liked her Mom, something Richard had never done. No she couldn't compare him to Richard, they were as different as night and day. When David introduced her to his friends and acquaintances he did so with pride, pleased with their relationship.

She knew that each day she was falling a little deeper in love with him. She hadn't told him that yet but she thought he might know. And she was sure his feelings for her were growing stronger as well. Soon she would have to confront him with her love for him. She hoped it wouldn't cause him to pull back.

She put the last of her clothes away and wandered through the house. He had indeed created a beautiful and private sanctuary, a setting where you could admire the natural beauty and feel secure and protected. He was trying to create that same environment at the B&B, to allow others to step out of their otherwise stressful existence and become immersed in a peaceful and relaxing setting. He wanted them to share the serenity he had found in the natural world of Alaska. She resolved to do her part in creating just such a Shangri-La.

CHAPTER 30

David dropped her off at the B&B the next morning. He knew she and Carolyn needed to discuss her roles and responsibilities without his involvement. He returned to the house and his home office while that occurred.

After a quick hug and enthusiastic welcome, the two got down to business. Meagan would assume complete responsibility for all financial aspects of Alaskan Adventures. She would maintain the books, create and track a budget, forecast income and expenses, and develop and present reports. Although she was responsible for the finances she would be expected to actively participate in discussion of all aspects of the management. She would be a full member of the executive team consisting of David, Carolyn, Jerry and now Meagan. The group met for two hours every

Monday morning to plan next steps and review progress to date. The group operated on a consensual model with Carolyn having veto power if the group couldn't reach agreement. To date that had never been necessary.

By the time they were fully open for business there would be 20 other full and part time employees involved in the landscaping, maintenance, housekeeping, food service, activities, and administration aspects. Currently there were four people employed part time and they would quickly move to full time and be in charge of their individual areas. The plan was to have a one-to-one ratio of employees to guests to attain the desired level of service.

The LLC had been set up with the capability of issuing shares. David held majority ownership. Meagan would receive a percentage of the ownership and profits as did both Carolyn and Jerry. It was the intent to have all full time employees participate in the profit sharing at some point in the future to further incent the desired levels of performance and behavior.

Meagan would initially start at half time although that was expected to increase to full time within 90 days. She could develop her own work schedule and let Carolyn know but she needed to plan to be here for the management team meetings on Mondays. She would receive an annual starting salary of $48,000 an amount that would double when she went to full time. Management was paid monthly while hourly staff was paid weekly. She would be covered by health, disability and life insurance and receive four weeks of paid vacation annually when she went to full time. A personal laptop and phone would be provided and there were printers, copiers and other equipment available in the administration office. She would have her own office as well. A contract had been developed to this effect and Carolyn handed her a copy for her approval and signature.

Oh, one other item came to mind. For the next couple of months, if desired, Meagan could use the Subaru Outback, one of the LLC's vehicles, that was parked in the garage. When they opened on a full time basis the vehicle would be needed for other purposes and she could make arrangements for her own transportation. Did she have any questions?

Meagan was amazed at the brisk efficiency with which everything had been presented. It all sounded satisfactory to her and after reading through the contract she signed it and gave it to Carolyn. A copy was made and given to Meagan.

"Now, let me show you to your office so you can set up your work area and get up to speed."

Carolyn led her to an office that contained an L-shaped desk, bookcases, files, desk phone, laptop and a personal printer/copier/fax. She told her the office chair was a temporary one and that Meagan could pick her own out from an office supply store the next time she was in Anchorage. She would soon receive a business credit card for any expenses incurred in performing her duties. She handed her an iPhone and gave her the phone number. She told her the password for the laptop and gave instructions on how to access the existing financial records. When no questions were forthcoming she left her to explore things on her own.

Meagan spent the next few hours immersed in learning about the financial records. She reviewed the expenses to date, the forecast for income and expenses going forward, and read the mission statement, goals and objectives for the business. She was impressed with what she saw. Everything was set forth in detail and seemed to be moving forward. They had decided to be an all Mac office and she approved. The accounting was done in QuickBooks. She was familiar with it since she used it for her own personal bookkeeping and assumed she would be able to hit the ground running.

CHAPTER 31

It was nearly 1 pm when there was a knock on her door. David stuck his head in and asked if she planned to take a break for lunch. She glanced at her watch. The time had gone by quickly. Rising from her chair she stretched a bit and went to meet him.

"I never turn down an invitation from a handsome man."

"I thought we could go down to Fat Olive's and grab a quick bite. You might as well start getting to know all the local hangouts and meeting the folks."

She quickly shut down her computer and joined him. They drove down the hill to the restaurant. David introduced her to the staff and said she'd be working at the B&B. The people welcomed her to Homer as they took their order. Meagan ordered halibut and David a small pizza. The place was full and most appeared to be locals.

Meagan filled him in on the position that had been given to her. She was impressed with what she had seen of the organization and how it operated. She was absorbing as much as she could so she would be able to be a good contributor to discussions. She was excited about the prospect and it showed.

"So what are you going to be doing in your spare time since it's only half time to start?"

"I think I'll poke around Homer and the surroundings a bit. I'll have the Outback available so you'll be able to do what you need without worrying about taking me places. I really want to get back into photography seriously again and explore my creative side. It's been a while since I did that. And I think I'd like to get back into painting again. I haven't done much along those lines since my undergrad days at UCLA."

"I talked with my sister today. She and the kids are coming up next week. Maybe you can spend some time showing them around a little bit. I'm anxious for her to meet you."

"I'd love to meet all of them as well. What are they like?"

David told her Linda was two years older than he. Meagan already knew Linda had gotten pregnant at 15, married the father and left home, and six years later had divorced.   She was now a single mother with two teenaged children, a girl and a boy. Alicia was 17 and a senior in high school. Kevin was 15 and a sophomore. Linda had had a tough time of things. Her marriage had been rocky from the start. Her husband had been emotionally abusive, drank heavily, and blamed Linda because he hadn't been able to go on to college and a better life. Apparently he hadn't considered he had an equal responsibility in the pregnancies. David hadn't been sorry when they divorced but he had regretted it as he had watched his sister retreat into herself.

To her credit, Linda had turned things around and moved forward with her life. She worked days and put herself through some online schooling and now had a job with the County of Ventura in their animal control division. She handled a lot of their administrative stuff, wasn't involved directly with the animals herself. He was proud of her and what she'd done. Her road had been bumpy but she hadn't complained. When David had come into his wealth she had steadfastly refused to accept anything from him. She wanted to do things on her own. She had allowed him to make the down payment on their house so she could finally have her own home for the kids. That was done as a personal loan on which she made regular monthly payments. He deposited all her payments in an account he had set up to help with the kids' college expenses should they decide to go. He hadn't told Linda that yet.

Alicia and Kevin were good kids and he enjoyed spending time with them. Alicia was very good looking and smart. He was glad he didn't have to deal with all the attention she was receiving from boys. She seemed interested in computers and technology and was planning on continuing her education but whether it would be to college or some kind of trade school she hadn't decided. Kevin didn't seem as academically inclined. He was more interested in machines and how things worked. He liked the outdoors and went camping whenever he had the chance. He had gotten in a little trouble a couple of times, had shoplifted some things and been caught smoking dope, and had been put on probation. David had a heart to heart talk with him at one point about adding to his mother's already stressful life and Kevin had made good on his promise to straighten up. It was clear David really liked both of the kids.

"I'd love to spend time with them and get to know all of them. Will they be staying at the house with us?"

"I thought about having them stay at the house but with Alicia's emerging sexuality I don't want her to get any more ideas than she already has. So I'm going to put them up at the B&B."

"They will enjoy it there. Carolyn and Jerry will fuss over them and they'll have the chance to see what you've created."

The week passed quickly. Meagan had settled into a routine where she worked each morning and spent the afternoon exploring Homer. Despite it being such a small town there were a lot of events taking place and things to do. It was nice having her own transportation and able to set her own pace. She found herself taking lots of pictures of both the scenery and the people.

CHAPTER 32

David and Meagan drove up to Anchorage to pick up Linda and the kids. They did some shopping before the group arrived. Meagan picked out a chair for her office and made arrangements for it to be delivered to Homer the following week. She picked up a few additional things for her office to suit her working style.

They waited in the baggage claim area for their arrival. When they walked in there were exclamations of "Uncle David" and all three embraced him in a welcoming hug. Meagan watched the genuine affection and warmth as it unfolded. Her relationships with her siblings and their families was nowhere near as demonstrative and she wondered why that was so.

David introduced the three to Meagan. Linda embraced her warmly and said she had been looking forward to meeting her. Alicia appraised her a moment and then hugged her as well. Kevin seemed unsure of how to balance his family's affectionate nature with a woman he didn't know. With a teenage boy's awkwardness he first extended his hand then relented when Meagan pulled him to her for a hug. He smiled shyly and hemmed and hawed a bit.

They retrieved the luggage and piled into David's Jeep. Kevin took the front seat with David and Meagan joined the females in the back seat. On the drive back to Homer David played tour guide and pointed out all the sights. This was the first trip to Alaska for any of them and their eyes were wide with amazement and excitement as the spectacular scenery unfolded.

When they passed the turnoff to Hope followed by the entrance to the Kenai Princess Lodge Meagan was aware of the intense feelings they evoked. So much had happened in such a short time since she had first come to the area. David glanced in the rearview mirror and quietly smiled his support. The conversation focused mostly on the sights they were absorbing. When they passed over the Kenai River and saw the waters dotted with fishing boats Kevin asked if they would be able to go fishing. David said he was sure something could be arranged.

They approached Homer and turned off on Diamond Ridge Drive. David drove past the turnoff to his house and instead took them directly to the B&B. Carolyn and Jerry greeted them as they entered the garage. When they entered the main room and saw the view that unfolded they gaped.

"Awesome," Kevin finally muttered. "That's freakin' awesome."

Linda and Alicia concurred with his opinion. A golf cart took them and the luggage to their cabin. Linda and Alicia would share the bed in the bedroom and Kevin would have the sofa bed in the living area it was decided. Kevin investigated the mini-fridge that had been stocked with juices, water and soft drinks and found its contents to his liking. They were left to unpack and freshen up and would meet in the main room of the lodge when they were ready. Jerry was preparing a welcoming dinner and he and Carolyn would join everyone for the meal.

David and Meagan walked back to the lodge hand in hand. The golf cart had been taken back earlier by one of the staff. Linda had stood at the door watching them walk back before turning to unpack her things.

The dinner was excellent and everyone complimented Jerry on the results. Kevin asked if they could cook any fish if he caught them. Jerry assured him of it and said he'd teach him a few tricks of the trade if he liked. David said he was tied up most of tomorrow but would have them over to his house for dinner that night. He told them Meagan would show them around Homer the next afternoon and bring them to the house for dinner. The trio returned to their cabin shortly after dinner. They had arisen early in Ventura and it had been a long day of traveling.

Meagan and David drove back home in his car, leaving hers at the B&B. He would drop her off in the morning on his way into town for some business. She commented on how glad Linda and her kids had been to see David.

"I was really pleased to see them as well. They are special people in my life and I care for them a lot. I don't get to see them as often as I would like so anytime we can manage to get together is great. Particularly now because it won't be long until the kids will be off on their own."

She noted that she had never heard him use the word love in reference to anyone, not his sister, the kids, nor had he said it to her. She could tell he loved Linda and the kids. But he seemed to be uncomfortable with the word and the concept. She was going to have to tell him soon of her love for him, he needed to know how she felt. She wanted to figure out how best to do it so he didn't panic at the thought.

CHAPTER 33

Meagan picked Linda and the kids up shortly after noon and took them down to Finn's Pizza for lunch. As they ate they watched the hustle and bustle of the fishing boats going in and out. They saw eagles fly past scanning the water below for their next meal. After lunch they drove out East End road as she showed them the sights. Kevin was enthralled with all the places he saw to go fishing. Alicia seemed to like the boutique stores in the quaint downtown area and was interested in the college. Meagan thought she might have to get Alicia by herself and bring her down here and get to know her. They drove to the overlook and admired the view. They went down to the beach and walked around. It was a pleasant and relaxing afternoon.

Shortly after 5 they arrived at David's house. He

was already in the kitchen preparing their meal. Linda and the kids exclaimed over the view. David had put some music on that was more upbeat for the kids who probably weren't aware there was music as they logged into the internet and played games on his laptop.

David grilled hamburgers and prepared a salad. While they were eating he said he was free tomorrow and would plan to take Kevin and Alicia out in the boat and they might even get a little fishing in. Linda politely declined David's offer to include her and said she'd see everyone when they returned. She wanted to have some time to get to know Meagan a little better and sensed this would be a good opportunity.

Shortly after noon the next day Linda knocked on Meagan's office door. Going inside she asked if they might have lunch a little later and get some time to chat. Meagan said she'd come by Linda's cabin at 1 and they could go from there.

When she arrived at the cabin Linda was sitting in a rocker on the porch. Jerry had prepared lunch for them and she brought it out and sat it on the small table between them. She helped herself to a sandwich and some fruit.

"How did you and David meet?"

"Do you want the short version or the long one?"

"Near as I figure we've got the whole afternoon."

Meagan told her of her voyage to Alaska and all the strange circumstances she had experienced. She told her of meeting David by the river and realizing she had already seen him in her dream. She told of the instant attraction and connection both had felt and how they both wanted to see where it would lead. She said she'd canceled the balance of her itinerary and come to Homer. Carolyn had offered her a job and she'd accepted. She and David had gone to San Diego to take care of her affairs and now she was here. She said she'd never before acted so rashly or impulsively.

"But you're glad you did."

"Yes, I'm glad I did. I still don't know where all this is going but I'm along for the ride."

"How long have you known you're in love with David?"

Meagan glanced over at Linda. She didn't see any disapproval in her face, just curiosity and concern.

"I realized it the second time we made love. The first time he made love to me and took me through feelings and sensations I didn't know I had inside of me. That night he held me the entire night. I don't think I've ever experienced something quite so intimate or ever felt so cherished. The second time he allowed me to give to him. I'd never felt such a personal connection with anyone before. I knew then in my heart that I loved him."

"Has he told you he loves you?"

"No. Nor have I told him how I feel."

"If I may ask, why haven't you told him?"

"My gut reaction is when I tell him it will frighten him. There's a part of him it feels like he keeps back from me, maybe from everyone. I want to tell him but I don't want to put roadblocks between us. I just want to continue to enjoy what we share."

Linda nodded as if she understood.

"Let me tell you a little about our childhood. I've never shared any of this with another woman that David has known. I think what he has with you is different than anything he's ever experienced. You need to know this if you want to truly know him."

"David's shared a little bit with me."

"I don't think he realizes how profoundly our mother affected him."

Linda told her their parents had divorced when David was four years old. She talked of the various relationships her mother had and how none of them lasted very long. They just packed up and moved from one place to another, one man to another. She said how she and David would just start to get close to someone and feel a little bit secure and then it would end and they'd be off to the next place and person.

She told of how much her mother and father hated each other. Many people who divorced didn't like each other but this was an unreasonably intense hatred. Their father hadn't been allowed to visit them at all.

Linda said that both of them had been distraught by this type of life but it had seemed to hurt David the most. He had desperately wanted to have a father figure in his life but they came and went. She, on the other hand, had craved any male attention. When it came it often had strings and so she had given sex in exchange for what she thought was love. When she ended up pregnant and left the house her mother had apparently had enough of child rearing. She contacted their father, a person she hated passionately, and told him his son would be there soon on a bus. David hadn't understood why she would send him away to be with someone she loathed. She just sort of vanished from their lives.

Linda found that the person she thought she loved really only wanted sex. Kevin had come along by then and he didn't want the hassle of raising children. Soon he was drinking heavily. Their relationship deteriorated to the point they were barely civil to each other. When she could see how badly the home environment was affecting Alicia and Kevin she packed up and left. She divorced their father and proceeded to raise them herself. She wasn't sorry she'd gotten married because having the kids was worth the cost.

She didn't think David had fared quite so well. When she and David had been together with their mother the two were inseparable. They took care of each other. If one of the men currently in her mother's life wanted to punish one of them he had to punish both. David lost that support when she left the house to get married. The next thing he knew he was on his way to his father's. He put on a good front but she knew he kept a lot bottled up inside.

Linda had known how badly she needed to leave home and she managed to make it happen. She hadn't realized how badly her leaving David would affect him.

"You seem to have made it through all this pretty well," Meagan commented.

"It took some time. I finally managed to put things in perspective and realized I had to let go of the frustration and anger. It wasn't easy but I managed to do it."

"Are you close to either of your parents?"

"Surprisingly to me I'm closer to my mother than my father. I've really never gotten to know him nor he me. I know he helped David a lot, and I'm grateful to him for that, but we don't seem to have anything in common. Maybe I'm just angry with him for leaving us to fend for ourselves."

"David said he hadn't spoken to his mother in three years."

"That's probably true. I don't know what went on between the two of them but something happened. Mother and I don't talk about David. It's as if the subject is taboo." She continued on, "At heart he's a very kind and generous person. He keeps a lot bottled up but I know it's there. When he sold his business he tried to buy a house for me and the kids. We agreed he could loan me the down payment not give it to me. I'm paying him back."

"Did you know he's putting the payments in a college fund for Alicia and Kevin?"

Linda laughed. "Doesn't surprise me. We're both pretty stubborn and he's determined to share his well being with me. We'll deal with it when we come to it."

Linda turned and took Meagan's hands in her own. "Be kind to him, Meagan. He's a good man and deserves to find happiness. He just needs to learn that loving and being loved doesn't have to hurt. You're the first person I've met who I think has a chance of helping him understand that."

David and the kids returned a short while later. Kevin grinned from ear to ear as he proudly showed them the fillets from the halibut he had caught. It had weighed about 22 pounds and they would be having it for dinner. He had to go over and help Jerry prepare it. With the bag of fillets in hand he left for the kitchen. Alicia had been enthralled with the wildlife they had seen. They had seen gulls and eagles and otters and walrus. She hadn't gotten seasick at all, even when the boat rocked when they stopped to fish.

CHAPTER 34

That night Meagan and David were lying in each other's arms. Their lovemaking had been especially tender and satisfying. Meagan took his face in her hands and watched his eyes as she spoke.

"I've fallen in love with you David. No, don't pull back. I'm not telling you to put any strings or obligations on you. I know you aren't ready to say that to me and that's okay. If and when you are I'll hear it then. But I know my heart and what I'm feeling. And I need to be able to share it with you because I want to be open and share everything. It doesn't have to change anything between us."

But she knew it would change things. At least it changed them for her. She had said the words before to a couple of men but she knew she had never before meant them like she did now. Whatever the future may bring she had found the man she wanted to share it with.

David was unsure how to respond. He knew he cared deeply for Meagan. And if he was honest with himself he had known she was falling in love with him. Did he love her? He honestly didn't know if he was capable of love. He didn't know if he was capable of opening himself up that much to anybody, not even himself. He leaned over and kissed her.

"Good night, Meagan."

"Good night, David. I love you."

The time passed quickly and soon Linda and her kids had returned to Ventura. David had put them on a plane in Homer and they connected in Anchorage to their flight to Los Angeles. It had been pleasant spending time with them and Meagan found she missed having them around.

Their days had settled into a comfortable routine. In the mornings Meagan would spend her time working. In the afternoons, while David continued working, she would roam the countryside surrounding Homer. She took pictures of all she saw and had captured some really interesting shots. She experimented with the various settings on her camera to try and achieve the effects she desired. She was glad she had decided to pursue her interest in photography again. In the evenings they would relax, often over a glass of wine, and share their day. She enjoyed the time they spent together but she also valued the time she had to herself.

She continued to periodically tell David that she loved him. It had become easier for her to say and she thought he was getting used to hearing it. At least now he didn't tighten up when she said the word aloud. She knew David loved her as well and was determined to help him become comfortable enough to tell her. Mostly she wanted to help him find the happiness he had brought to her life.

CHAPTER 35

At dinner one evening David asked Meagan if he'd told her about his friend Mark Freeman. He and David had played basketball together in high school and become good friends. During summers they had worked as laborers for his Dad. After high school they had gone their separate ways. When David headed off to USC Mark had enlisted in the Air Force. He had ended up working in air traffic control and his interest and love affair with flying had begun. After his four-year stint was over he had used his veteran's educational benefits to become a pilot. He became a flight instructor, went on mail runs and pursued his commercial pilot's license. He had carried passengers on charter flights but had never worked for a major airline. His vision, while good enough for flying, didn't meet the high standards required of pilots in today's marketplace. Most recently he'd been working in construction in Paso Robles but with the housing decline was taking a break and rethinking what he wanted to do. They had gotten together a few times after David sold his business but hadn't seen each other since he had come to Alaska.

Mark had sent him an email and inquired about coming up to visit for a while in Alaska. David wondered if Meagan would mind having him for a houseguest for a while as it would save Mark the cost of a motel. Meagan said it was fine with her and she would look forward to meeting another of his friends. She also thought it would be a good chance to get to know even more about David in his younger days.

Mark arrived the following week. He flew directly into Homer and David met him at the airport terminal. His luggage was quickly retrieved and they piled into David's Jeep and headed up to the house. Small talk was made as they caught up on friends and acquaintances.

Inside the house Mark was shown to his room and left to get settled. When he emerged a short time later Meagan had arrived home and the two were introduced. Mark was an inch or two shorter than David with long light brown hair tied back in a ponytail. Meagan thought many women would be jealous of his hair. He was lean and wiry and casually dressed in jeans and a flannel shirt. She thought he would fit in well with

Alaskan dress standards. Where David's eyes were a brilliant blue, Mark had soft green eyes. He was relaxed and pleasant and chatting with him was easy and comfortable.

Over dinner the conversation quickly turned to their high school days and basketball. She found out that in their senior year they had come in second in the state championship playoffs. Mark told her that he was the primary one responsible for David's basketball prowess.

"If I hadn't always fed him the ball he never would have scored so much and gotten the scholarship offer from USC. He owes it all to me."

"And if I hadn't managed to track down all the erratic passes you threw we'd never have won a single game. I saved your sorry butt!"

Meagan observed them as they continued their playful banter. They clearly had a lot of affection and respect for each other. She envied them their easygoing camaraderie. She tried to imagine them back in high school as teenagers. She found it easy to do. During summers they had both worked for David's father in construction. That was the experience Mark had been able to fall back on that when he couldn't find a job as a pilot. He said that with the downturn in the economy construction jobs had fallen on hard times and he'd barely worked in the last six months.

Afterwards as they sat by the fire with a cup of coffee she asked Mark what he hoped to do now.

"What I'd really like is to get back into flying. I enjoyed that more than anything I've ever done. I thought I'd see if there might be any openings available for bush pilots. I still have all my credentials up to date although I'm sure I'd need to take some classes on flying in the conditions routinely encountered up here. I've got a little money I've squirreled away and maybe I'll pick up my own plane if it looks like a viable proposition."

David suggested Mark swing by Homer Air tomorrow and talk with them. He said he knew Dave Rush, the current owner, and had negotiated with them to provide various services for Alaskan Adventures clientele. He said he'd give Dave a call in the morning and set something up and Mark could use the Jeep to go over.

When Meagan arrived home the next afternoon Mark had already met with Dave Rush. He said he was cautiously optimistic as Homer Air indicated they could always use good pilots. If he purchased his own plane it would be a definite advantage and he'd start looking around at what might be available. Meanwhile he'd start cranking out some numbers to see how it would all play out. She offered her services if he'd like in doing some projections. She explained her background in finance and told him what she was doing now up at the B&B. He said he'd be grateful for any help as numbers weren't his forte.

They talked about her relationship with David. Mark had watched the two of them the evening before and could see that this was serious. He recalled both he and David had dated a fair amount in high school but neither had what he'd term a steady relationship. He personally hadn't been inclined to settle down with one individual and David didn't seem to want to get too close to anyone. During his time in the Air Force he had moved from one place to another, none for more than a year, and had yet to meet that special person. He figured he was still pretty young and when it was time it would happen.

It was easy to talk with Mark. He was interested in and knowledgeable about a variety of topics. When he discovered Meagan's interest in photography he suggested she might want to accompany him when he went flying to explore this area. She would not only see things from a different perspective but flying in a small plane offered the chance to take pictures of places you couldn't otherwise reach and see. She said she'd love to do it.

The next Monday at their management team

meeting Meagan raised the issue of purchasing a plane and employing a pilot. She said she had reviewed the projected expenses budgeted for guest activities and wondered if they might not save money while acquiring an additional asset. If the group would like she'd run some numbers and send them out so they could talk in more depth at the next meeting. After getting the group's approval she added it to her task list.

CHAPTER 36

The following morning David had arisen early, as usual, and prepared breakfast. He had left Meagan and Mark sitting at the kitchen counter saying he had things to do in his office. When he came back in he picked up a dishtowel that had fallen to the floor muttering under his breath. He refilled his coffee cup and found only a small amount remained in the carafe.

"Damn it. Do I have to do everything around here?"

Meagan and Mark glanced at each other.

"Did someone get up on the wrong side of the bed this morning?" Mark inquired.

"At least I get up out of bed and do something. I don't lie around all the time like a bump on a log."

Meagan had had enough and waded into the fray. "As I recall you were the one who suggested Mark just relax and take it easy for a while. Now you don't like it that he is. Make up your mind."

"Nobody asked for your opinion."

Her temper flared and she replied back angrily, "No you didn't but I'm giving it anyway. Since you don't want to deal with things like the adult you're supposed to be maybe we should just treat you like a child. You're acting like a spoiled brat."

She glared at him and he glared back.

"I'll act any way I want. It's my house."

So it has come to that, she thought. She debated whether to respond in kind. Instead she switched gears.

"David, what's really bothering you?"

"It's my Dad. Something's wrong with his heart."

"Oh my God. Why didn't you say so in the first place? What is it? What's happened to him?"

"I don't have all the details. I just got a text message from Sally. He passed out on the front porch. She saw him fall when he went out to get the paper and called an ambulance. He's at the hospital in Northridge."

Mark, too, was concerned. David's father had been kind enough to give him a job as a general laborer during the summer after his sophomore year in high school. He had always appreciated it because that was how he got enough money to buy his first car. Besides, he liked and respected Ralph. And David was his friend.

"Do you want to go down there? Want me to make arrangements or anything?"

"Not yet. Sally said he's conscious and talking. She's with him at the hospital and will give me a call when she can. Don't know what I can do at the moment but wait to hear."

Meagan walked over to him and put her arms around him. She laid her head on his shoulders.

"I'm sorry, David. I know how helpless you must feel right now."

He suddenly remembered that only a short while ago Meagan's father had died of a heart attack. This must be really hitting close to home for her. He regretted his earlier outburst.

"I'm sure you must. Did your Dad ever regain consciousness after his heart attack?"

"No, he was declared dead by the time they got to the hospital. Mom never had a chance to tell him goodbye."

Mark got up and made coffee. They sat around the counter waiting for news. A short while later the phone rang and David put it on speakerphone. Sally said Ralph had been diagnosed with atrial fibrillation or a-fib. A drop in his blood pressure when his heart went out of rhythm had caused him to faint. They were putting him on a blood thinner to prevent the possibility of a stroke and running some other tests. They'd keep him comfortable and resting for a day or two to make sure his heart would remain in normal sinus rhythm. He had hit his head when he fell and had a nasty bump but everything else looked okay.

David asked if she wanted him to come down there. She said the she didn't think it was necessary from what the doctor told her about the condition. Perhaps he could give his Dad a call later on today when things settled down a bit. He agreed to do so and the call was disconnected.

"I apologize, guys, for getting upset with both of you. You didn't do anything. I was just worried. Regardless, it was still out of line."

"It's understandable given the circumstances," said Mark. "I'm really glad he's okay, David. I like your Dad a lot."

Meagan had wondered how they would handle any

issues that arose. She was surprised she had come to Mark's defense so quickly and had let her own temper get the best of her. But then David hadn't given any indication something was wrong and instead just lashed out. Maybe they were going to have to learn how to fight fair when something was wrong.

David researched atrial fibrillation on the web and was surprised to find how common it was among men his father's age. While it would require some medication and care it was not as critical as he had first feared. He called his Dad that afternoon and the two chatted pleasantly. He told him Mark was visiting and sent his regards. His Dad pooh poohed the episode but David could tell it had worried him just the same. They resolved to talk again in a couple of days once he had returned home.

CHAPTER 37

An unexpected surprise awaited Meagan the following day when she returned home from work. David's car was already in the garage, which was somewhat unusual for the middle of the day. When she walked through the door she was besieged by a black and white bundle of fur that was wagging its tail and licking her furiously. Upon closer examination she determined it had two bright blue eyes that contrasted sharply with the white and black markings surrounding them. David and Mark sat across the room grinning from ear to ear.

"What is this and where did it come from?" she asked.

"It's a puppy and it just left its mother."

"Obviously it's a puppy. I meant what is it doing

here."

"It's for you." David answered. "I thought you might like some companionship."

Meagan sat down beside the furry dynamo that quickly crawled into her lap. It was soft and cuddly and unbelievably cute. When she petted it the dog wriggled in enthusiastic ecstasy. She hadn't been around a dog since she left home to go to college. She had never had her own pet. Her parents had always preferred boxers. But this was no boxer. She knew it was a Siberian Husky from its black and white markings and blue eyes. It was beautiful. She loved it.

"David, it's adorable. How long have you been planning this?"

"Two weeks now. One of the guys I know raises sled dogs. He told me about his newest puppies and brought some pictures. I went to see them and this one just seemed to have your name on him. He's eight weeks old today so now he can leave the litter. Tomorrow we'll have been together for a month and it seemed a good way to commemorate it. Your Mom said you didn't have any allergies to dogs or anything like that."

"You called my Mom about a puppy?"

"Yeah, she thought you'd like one. Said to tell you

hello."

"You never cease to amaze me, David. I've always wanted to have a dog of my own. And now you've given that wish to me. Thank you." Meagan rose and kissed him tenderly on the cheek. "Does he have a name?"

"Not yet. You get to choose one for him."

She looked at the puppy who looked back and cocked his head.

"It's Diamond. My first gift from you is a diamond. He's shiny and beautiful just like the stone he's named after." Picking the puppy up she said, "I christen you Diamond." The puppy's tail beat furiously and he licked his approval.

They spent time that evening puppy-proofing part of the house. They brought newspapers into their bathroom where Diamond would spend the night and set about the training process.

To celebrate their one-month anniversary the next day David took Meagan to dinner at the Eagle's Crest Restaurant at the Kenai Princess Lodge. Mark had agreed to keep an eye on Diamond. It somehow seemed appropriate to return to the place where they first met. They shared an appetizer of Kenai salmon lettuce wraps. For an entrée she had the asiago crusted halibut and he chose the honey glazed salmon. They sipped wine from a bottle of Conundrum throughout. After dinner they walked down to the river where they had first embraced and kissed.

As their lips met he thought that he would never tire of kissing her. They did so every day and it always generated excitement for him. The softness of her lips seemed to invite deeper exploration and he applied himself willingly to the task. For herself she responded in kind. When his arms enveloped her it was if her own personal sanctuary was created. It was familiar now and comfortable but it still remained stimulating and electrifying.

"I love you, David." The emotion in her voice was powerful and seductive.

"My precious Meagan. My beautiful and wonderful Meagan."

Contented they stood together alongside the rock where she found the stone heart. She finally broke the silence.

"I keep thinking we're supposed to be doing something to fulfill this prophecy but I don't know what to do. Is there something we're missing?"

"I think we're already on the path to making it happen. It's been waiting for a long time now and I don't think it has to be done overnight."

She relaxed at his words. That was what she wanted to believe as well. She just needed to be able to trust the process and allow it to move at its own pace.

CHAPTER 38

David was confused. The relationship with Meagan had brought a measure of comfort and fulfillment to his life. It just felt so good and so right. He knew it had been lacking before. But still he couldn't stop wondering if he was doing the right thing. The more he spent time with her the more he wanted to be with her. When would the bad stuff happen? He knew everything couldn't be a bed of roses. Life wasn't like that at all. He'd seen it happen over and over before.

She had already worked her way deeper and deeper inside of him. He knew it but didn't know how to not let it happen. He also knew she could hurt him, hurt him badly, if she chose to do so. It scared him to think about it. He had gotten good before at not letting himself be caught in this position. If he didn't let anyone inside he had nothing to worry about. They couldn't hurt him if they didn't get in.

Making love with Meagan was like nothing he had ever experienced before. Oh, he'd enjoyed sex previously with a number of women. And it had been pleasurable and exciting and fun. He knew he was a good lover and he enjoyed pleasing a woman. And he liked it when a woman pleased him. Yes, sex felt good. But being with Meagan was beyond good. It was out of this world. He could tell she was satisfied and fulfilled afterwards. She told him he'd brought out sensations and feelings she'd never known before. And if he were honest she did the same for him. He'd never experienced anything so exhilarating as he did when they made love. Yet it could still be tender and gentle while also intense. He wondered what it would be like if they weren't so gentle with each other. He found the thought arousing.

So what were his options? Basically he could choose to stay involved with her or he could choose not to be involved. Those were the choices. It was as simple as that. Yet it wasn't simple at all. If she left him he'd be devastated. But wouldn't he also be devastated if he left her? Would it hurt any less if he was the one who left? How in the world had he managed to get himself into this predicament? He was damned if he did and damned if he didn't.

That afternoon he was sitting in Carolyn's office

discussing business. He trusted Carolyn. She was a good listener and a good friend. He decided to ask her what she thought of all this. He shared with her the dilemma he felt confronted him and waited for a response.

Carolyn had thought David must be going through just such a process internally. She knew a little about his background with his mother and his skepticism about relationships. She also knew how much more alive and positive and energized he'd been since he and Meagan had been together. She listened patiently while he voiced his concerns and thought about what she might say to him that would have the meaning she wanted.

"Has Meagan given any indication that she might want to leave or somehow change the relationship?"

"No, but that doesn't mean it couldn't happen."

"That's true. And that's always a risk with anything. That it might not last or turn out to be different than you had wanted. But it seems to me that if you spend all your time worrying about what might happen you don't get to experience and enjoy what is happening. How do you feel when you're with her?"

"I feel relaxed and peaceful and contented. I feel good."

"How do you think Meagan feels when you're together?"

"The same way. She's told me that when we hold each other that it is her safe spot in the world."

"Relationships don't have to be a struggle, David. You're not in competition with each other. One of you doesn't have to win and the other lose. You can both win. That's what happens in a good relationship. You both win." She continued on, "Do you believe in positive and negative energy?"

"Yes."

"So do I. And I believe that you can influence the outcome of things by what you choose to focus on. I would urge you to focus on the positive energy in your relationship rather than any potential negative."

"Thanks, Carolyn. I always feel better when we talk."

"I enjoy it as well, David. I care about you a great deal. You're not just the owner to me. You're my friend as well."

CHAPTER 39

At the management team the following Monday the group evaluated Meagan's proposal and decided to move forward with purchasing an airplane and hiring a pilot. David was put in charge and would locate and purchase an airplane, hire a pilot and negotiate with Homer Air to sell them any excess capacity. He had presented Mark's background and capabilities and all felt he would be a good fit with the organization.

Meagan, however, wasn't through presenting her thoughts just yet. She outlined ideas for ways to enhance options for guests by expanding past simply offering activities. She suggested incorporating indigenous culture, art and history. Educational and volunteer opportunities could be made available, possibly for college credit. Businesses could be approached about corporate retreats themed around outdoor activities and team building. She said she'd be putting together details on each of these areas and would bring them to the group for discussion at subsequent meetings.

David called Mark and said he'd like to sit down and talk with him. They agreed to meet at the house for lunch. While they ate he laid out Meagan's idea for Alaskan Adventures purchase of an airplane and hiring of a pilot. He showed him the figures about how they would be able to expand their transportation services and activities. While it would cost a little more than they had originally forecast, the increases would be more than offset by the acquisition of an asset and tax write-offs associated with it. When they didn't have flights scheduled they would be available to conduct flights for Homer Air. He asked if Mark would be interested in being their pilot and assisting him in the purchase of the equipment. Mark didn't even pause before accepting. At last he would be able to get back to doing something he loved.

Mark used David's home office as his base to begin his search for an appropriate aircraft. He powered up his laptop and logged on to the web. Diamond had come in to help in the search and he absentmindedly reached down and scratched the puppy's ears. The puppy promptly curled up at his feet and fell asleep.

His research revealed that one of the best bush

airplanes available would be a refurbished De Havilland DHC-3 Otter. The planes were originally built in the 1950's and 1960's and only 466 were made. Capable of holding 9-10 passengers in addition to two pilots, the planes could be fitted with floats, skis or just the wheels. The original models with their Pratt & Whitney engines were considered a bit underpowered and some had been retrofitted with Polish PZL 1000 hp radial engines. New the plane had sold for $145,000 but today a good refurbished one, particularly one with the updated engine, would be in the $850,000 range. Still, that was a lot less than buying a brand new plane and the rugged nature and short take off and landing capability provided by the Otter was superior. He prepared a justification for his choice and set about locating any that might be available for purchase.

After several hours of web searching and phone calls Mark wondered if he might have to reconsider his recommendation as there were few of the Otters for sale. Finally he located a company in Yellowknife in the North West Territories of Canada that was closing its doors and had one available. A phone call to the owner revealed that the Otter was still for sale. He conveyed his interest and the owner agreed to email him some pictures and detailed information. The asking price was $900,000 Canadian.

That evening Mark reviewed the materials with David. Both felt it sounded like an ideal aircraft for their needs. They called and set up an appointment with the owner and made arrangements to fly to Calgary and connect to Yellowknife on the following day.

David called his Dad since he would be leaving in the morning to find out how he was doing. Other than complaining about Sally fussing over him he said he was doing fine. His a-fib seemed to be under control with the medications he'd been put on and he hoped to get back to his regular activities soon. David told him of the decision to purchase an aircraft and his trip the next day to Yellowknife.

CHAPTER 40

Meagan found herself filling her afternoons and evenings fleshing out the details of expanding guest options. The more she investigated, the more excited she became at the kinds of experiences they would be able to create for the people who came to partake of all Alaskan Adventures could offer. Because of what had occurred with her she wanted others to be able to recognize their totem and select activities that would help them explore it further. She found programs available through the local Pratt Museum whereby the peoples of Kachemak Bay, local marine and land-based animals, and the surrounding forest ecology could be brought to life for visitors. They would learn of the history of the area from its original inhabitants to its occupation by Russian fur traders to the influx of American gold-seekers. She sought out remote communities that still today practiced a sustenance style existence.   She identified local residents, including Native Americans, who were knowledgeable about these topics and who would be available to teach and present.   After working in the office during the mornings, then researching during the afternoon, she would make copious notes during the evenings as her research progressed.   She found herself ignoring her photography as she immersed herself in the tasks she had set for herself.

Satisfied with her efforts to date on incorporating a local flavor, she then turned her attention to educational offerings.   She put together outlines for classes on photography, writing and self-publishing that guests could select.   There were so many resources already available online.   Guests already booked could even choose to take and complete some before they arrived, thereby preparing them for and involving them in their trip before it even happened.   She met with representatives from Kenai Peninsula College to see about offering credits for the classes and activities.   She discussed setting up an internship program for students to both learn and work at the lodge and on activities.

During the summer with the nearly 24 hour growing season, fruits and vegetables flourished in Alaska.   She worked with Jerry to develop field trips to local farmer's markets or the nearby wilds to gather berries and nuts.   He would then offer culinary classes to teach them how to prepare the foods they had gathered or the fish they had caught. The emphasis would always be on using fresh local ingredients.

She located opportunities for participating in trail maintenance and wilderness preservation with the Division of Parks & Outdoor Recreations through the Alaskan Department of Natural Resources. At nearby hatcheries people could assist in raising and releasing fry to keep salmon runs populated. They would get a first hand look at nature and all it took to sustain it. They would gain an appreciation beyond what was there on the surface.

Everywhere she looked and turned Meagan found herself becoming more and more caught up in the Alaska that had so captivated David. It wasn't just the scenic beauty and grandeur. It was the people, their outlook and approach to life. It was the shared beliefs and values of its inhabitants. It felt different and more inclusive. When you combined it all together it made you feel welcome and accepted. But you had to work, and work hard at it, for it wasn't forgiving. If you made mistakes you could pay for them, even die from them. It could be cold and cruel at the same time it was accepting and giving. All in all it was a contradiction. A conundrum, that's what it was, a conundrum. And Meagan loved mysteries and solving them.

CHAPTER 41

David returned alone from the trip to Yellowknife. They had made arrangements to purchase the Otter and the seller would cover the costs of having it flown to Homer. When he saw the pristine condition in which it had been maintained he hadn't haggled much over the price. Mark would accompany the pilot on the trip to better familiarize himself with the aircraft. The skis, pontoons and some additional spare parts would be shipped to Homer by truck and would be here in a little over a week. He made arrangements to have the Otter kept in a hangar at Homer Air.

When he arrived home he found Meagan absorbed in her writing. Diamond was curled up at her feet. She hadn't heard him come in and he watched her for a few minutes as she concentrated on the tasks at hand, scrunching up her face and twisting her hair in her hands.

"Some watchdog that dog turned out to be," he announced himself from the doorway. "I could have snuck up and had my way with you some time ago."

"You, sir, can have your way with me anytime you want," she said as she rose, smiling, to greet him. "How was the trip back?"

He assured her it had been fine but long. They had spoken each day on the phone and she knew he had purchased the aircraft. Now there was just the two of them for a couple of days before Mark arrived back with the Otter.

She stepped into his arms. "I missed you, David. I missed being with you, looking at you, talking with you. I missed holding you and being held by you. And I missed this," she said as she tilted her face up and kissed him.

He had been tired and irritable and grouchy when he had driven up. It was amazing how quickly those feelings vanished as he savored the kiss. He liked tasting her, touching her, and smelling her. The trip had been a success and he had enjoyed getting some quality time with Mark, but this is where he wanted to be, he realized.

He asked how she'd been and she shared all the

things she'd been working on. She had told him a little about it when they'd talked on the phone but now he could see the sparkle in her eyes and hear the excitement in her voice. He sat in a chair and pulled her onto his lap. They fit comfortably together and he listened attentively as she told him of her endeavors.

"It sounds to me like you're completing a circle, creating a whole out of all the parts, allowing people to see the many facets of Alaska and how they fit together."

"I know they won't have time to do everything. I just want them to be able to find something that initially intrigues them and then leads them to understanding it is just a piece of a bigger whole. There is so much to see and absorb."

"It's a good thing we managed to catch you before the Alaska Chamber of Commerce snapped you up."

"I remember when you first told me of Alaskan Adventures and Kachemak View B&B and what you were trying to create. You had the body and skeleton already put together and now we can bring it to life. I'm so excited about this."

He marveled at the transition that had occurred in Meagan. There was so much more she was capable of than simply manipulating numbers. Oh, she was good at that as well as she'd demonstrated when preparing the cost benefit analysis of purchasing an airplane. But there was a whole creative side of her as well that took joy in assembling something whole from disparate pieces. Isn't that what he also enjoyed? It was the process of transforming an idea into reality that brought him the most satisfaction. How strange that someone with a conservative fiscal background should also feel that way. He had not expected that from her. But he liked it.

She told him one of the things she had yet to address is how to best position Alaskan Adventures to offer services tailored for businesses. She was kicking around some ideas for how they could provide corporate retreats that focused on team building activities and used what they learned to solve real problems. If they could get a foothold in that market they could not only generate a lot of income but help influence the values driving businesses. And if they could get one or two major companies to use them the word would spread. Her enthusiasm was contagious.

"Seems like we're wasting you in finance. You need to be in marketing."

"David, it's all tied together. If you want to bring about change you have to get inside of what you want to change. You can't simply stand outside and criticize. That's what protesters and picketers don't understand. Sometimes they're necessary too, but all they really do is increase awareness of the problem. Real change happens from within. If we can get inside of some of these businesses and help them solve problems they are running up against we can influence the way they do business. Oh, I'm so glad you gave me the chance to help with this."

"So am I, Meagan." He held her tightly against him. "So am I."

CHAPTER 42

Mark returned with the Otter and spent a lot of his time becoming familiar with various places they would be flying the guests to participate in activities. He had scheduled a trip to Talkeetna to go through bush pilot and float plane training with Above Alaska Aviation. His prior flying experience was valuable but this would be the best method of quickly preparing him for some of the Alaskan conditions he would encounter. He would be up there for a week. He did not take the Otter as the company provided aircraft for the courses. Upon his return home he would adapt his newfound skills to the Otter.

The days were filled with activity as they prepared to actually open Alaskan Adventures and the B&B for business. Additional staffing had been added and training was in progress. The management team had wholeheartedly embraced Meagan's ideas and she continued to spend her afternoon and evenings finalizing the details for incorporation into the overall program. The following week would find the first paid guests arriving and in two weeks they were planning a grand opening celebration. Their website was up and running and was garnering a good deal of attention from interested searchers. As with anything there were some small hiccups but for the most part it was all proceeding smoothly and on schedule.

When Mark returned from his training he began devoting more and more time to transferring his skills to the Otter. One morning he approached Meagan and asked if she'd like to join him that afternoon for a flight to the Native Village of Nanwalek located across the Kachemak Bay from Homer. He wanted to practice some takeoffs and landings at the type of rural locations he would be shuttling guests to for activities. When she readily agreed he told her to make sure she packed her camera.

She met Mark at Homer Air and was impressed with his attention to detail as he conducted his safety check of the Otter. He was clearly a careful and conscientious pilot. He noted her watching him and commented that it was best to catch any potential issues on the ground as they were more difficult to deal with when only air surrounded them. She concurred wholeheartedly. They were soon airborne for the short flight across Kachemak Bay.

The Nanwalek Airport has an airport designator of KEB and used to be called English Bay. Comprised of packed gravel and only 1850 feet long it is considered the shortest runway in the USA used by US commuter airlines. It averages 8 flights per day, the vast majority of which are commuters. There are no navigational aids and pilots on approach must keep their eyes peeled for ATVs that are frequently seen on the runway. The flight over was enjoyable and Mark executed a smooth landing. Once they landed Meagan deplaned and looked around.

The Native people of Nanwalek call themselves Sugpiaq meaning "real people". Their heritage is strongly based in their language, subsistence lifestyle, cultural traditions and self-government. Their culture has steadfastly survived the Russian and later American impact on traditional lifestyles.

Meagan had begun snapping pictures while Mark did his pre-flight inspection and she continued to take them during the flight and on the ground. There was not a lot to see in Nanwalek. The people here lived primarily from what they could harvest from the sea or reap from the land. She thought she would like to come back sometime and meet some of the people who lived this way. She knew they held some local celebrations and resolved to try and schedule one in.

They returned to Homer and Mark secured the airplane. They drove out onto the spit and got out to walk around. Meagan continued to take pictures of boats unloading the days catch while birds circled overhead looking for scraps. There were pelicans perched on pilings storing energy for their next flight. In one location she saw a young Native American man who sat on a rock staring at the sea around him. The sky was gray and overcast and his mood seemed to mirror the sky. She zoomed in and took some close-ups as they walked past. She continued to take pictures of the waterfront, shops and people as they strolled along the spit.

Mark drove her back to the house and she thanked him for a pleasant and relaxing afternoon. It had been good to break her routine, clear her head, and get away for a few hours. Now she could get back into the swing of things with renewed energy and purpose.

Alaskan Adventures and the Kachemak View B&B opened without fanfare. Only six paying guests were scheduled for the first few nights. They had been selected because they afforded a good cross-section of needs and interest in activities. Although a few hiccups occurred during their stays they were transparent to the guests themselves and quickly corrected.

The careful planning and attention to detail they had put in to offer a comprehensive Alaskan experience was rewarded. Jerry received rave reviews for the cuisine. Mark ferried guests to Katmai National Park for bear watching while others went halibut fishing with David. Meagan gave a brief workshop on digital photography and then led three individuals on a guided photo shoot on the spit and out the East End road. Four of the guests attended a presentation on totems and their meaning and identified the animal belonging to them. A visit to a Native American gallery and store in Homer enabled them to purchase souvenir totems. At night the guests relaxed around a campfire and shared their experiences of the day while excitedly talking about what they would be doing next. The feedback they received from the initial clients was overwhelmingly positive. Some minor suggestions for improvements were made and readily incorporated into the operation.

The next major hurdle would be the grand opening. The opening day's activities would include a luncheon attended by the mayor of Homer and representatives from the local newspaper, TV channel and Kenai Peninsula College. Vendors, tour guides and others with whom they had business relationships had also been invited as well as a number of friends. For the kickoff they had a full house of guests booked for stays ranging from three days to an entire week.

CHAPTER 43

Diane had been communicating frequently with Meagan via email and phone calls. She was planning a visit and would arrive the day before the grand opening celebration. She was planning to spend a week but by carefully scheduling trial dates she might be able to extend that for a few days. She was also very curious about David and looking forward to meeting him firsthand. She would be staying with them in a spare bedroom at David's as the B&B was completely booked.

Meagan picked Diane up at the Anchorage airport to bring her back to Homer. She had previously returned the Subaru to the B&B since it was now in almost daily use and had purchased a Jeep Liberty from the dealer in Anchorage. This trip afforded her the opportunity to take it in for its initial servicing and that had already been performed. On their way out of town they stopped by the REI store on Northern Lights Boulevard so Diane could pick up some clothes more suited to her trip than her Southern California clothes. They were soon on their way back to Homer.

Meagan pointed out a number of sights as they drove past and filled Diane in on what she was seeing. As they drove along Turnagain Arm she explained how the bore tide came in creating large waves. The huge volume of water that came in from the incoming tide in Cook Inlet was funneled into an increasingly narrower area resulting in waves up to 10 feet in height when peak tidal conditions were present. Occasionally people even surfed the waves. When she thought about it she was amazed at how much she had absorbed in the two short months she had been in Alaska.

It was readily apparent to Diane that Meagan really liked it here. She hadn't seen her this outgoing and exuberant in a long time. Diane had minored in psychology and worked summer jobs as a counselor before entering law school but it didn't take any specialized knowledge or training to see her friend was in her element. She said so to Meagan.

"It's true. I absolutely love it here. I still have to pinch myself periodically to make sure it's real. And wait till you meet Diamond! He's the cutest thing. He's starting to grow into his feet a bit and he constantly tests his limits but he's just adorable."

"How's the job going?"

"It's great. The people I work with are just the nicest people. They listen to my ideas and discuss them and have incorporated a number of them into our program. I feel valued and respected for my ideas and what I contribute. You'll see for yourself when we get there. And you'll see how the community values what we're doing when we have the grand opening."

When they approached Cooper Landing Meagan turned off at the Kenai Princess Lodge and suggested a late lunch. A few minutes later they were seated in the dining room with a glass of wine waiting for their sandwiches.

"So this is where it all started?"

"It started before this on the voyage up. But, yes, this is where I first met David. I can't wait for you to meet him. He is just the most special man I've ever met. I know you're going to like him. Sometimes it's like I'm living in a dream."

Their food came and the conversation waned a bit as they dug in. Meagan asked about Diane's job and how her life was going.

"I think I'm going to have to find something else to do at some point. I'm making good money and don't know what I can do to keep that coming in. But the problem is I'm not enjoying it any longer. I can't imagine continuing to do something that doesn't bring me more than just the money. I guess we'll see what comes next."

"Any men in your life?"

"No one special. I go out occasionally but nothing's really clicked with anyone for a while. Honestly, I'm not sure how much fun I am to be with right now while I'm still trying to figure out where I want to go. I envy you the direction your life is heading."

"I'm really fortunate to have found David, my job, the whole situation. I feel so much better about me and what I'm doing than I ever did in San Diego. I'm not trying to rub it in but it's true. Did I tell you I sold the condo?"

"No. Congratulations. Is that the last of your ties to the area?"

"Pretty much. I still have family down there. And of course you are there, too. Slowly but surely it all seems to be coming together here. I'm truly grateful for what I have."

"So are you still in love with him?"

"Oh yes. My feelings keep growing stronger every

day. I don't know how they do but they do. The more I learn about him and the more we share the more attracted I am to him. It's really an overpowering sensation."

"And does he love you?"

"He hasn't said it in so many words but I know he does. It's in his eyes, his voice, the way he treats me, everything. But he isn't comfortable enough to tell me he loves me yet."

A couple of hours later they pulled into the garage at David's house and walked inside. Like everyone else who visited, Diane's mouth opened in awe as she walked to the window and looked at the picture postcard view that unfolded before her. Diamond had followed them across the room and she picked him up and stroked him. They retrieved her luggage and she was shown to her room. It didn't have the same views as the living room but it did look out to a grove of trees and natural landscaping. She unpacked and decided to take a quick nap to recover from the effects of the day's travel.

CHAPTER 44

She awakened nearly an hour later, freshened up a bit, and went into the living area. David and Mark had arrived home and were sitting at the breakfast bar talking quietly. Meagan was nowhere to be seen.

"I'm afraid Meagan needed to take Diamond outside for a bit," David said as he rose and introduced himself. "He hasn't mastered his potty training when he gets excited. Hello, Diane, I'm David. It's very nice to finally meet you in person because I've heard a lot of good things about you."

He took her hands in his and welcomed her to Alaska with a hug. He smiled with his eyes as well as his mouth she decided. He said he knew how glad Meagan was she had been able to come and visit. He was, too, because he had been looking forward to meeting her and knew how important her friendship was to Meagan.

"Besides," he said grinning, "I figure you're an integral part of bringing Meagan into my life because of your voyage. That's where I hear it all started."

He had a powerful and charismatic air about him that she felt most women would respond to and find very appealing. She did. He carried himself with an easy authority and confidence. His words rang of sincerity. She liked him, she decided. She had been prepared to like him for Meagan's sake regardless but she was glad she liked him for herself as well.

David turned and introduced her to Mark who also took her hands in his and welcomed her to Alaska in general and Homer in particular. He tried not to stare at her but found it difficult not to do so. He thought she was quite simply the most beautiful woman he had ever met in his life. Meagan had told him Diane was good looking but she had never prepared him to be confronted by such a divine being. His mind raced as he searched for ways he might spend time with her. It sounded pretty lame to him but he told her he flew visitors on many of the organization's tours and would be happy to show her around.

Diane was amused by Mark's consternation. She was aware of her looks and the effect she had on men.

While she wasn't vain about her appearance she also wasn't above taking advantage of it in the courtroom and her practice. She knew David noticed her looks but coolly controlled his response and didn't react to them nor comment on them.

Mark, on the other hand, displayed his reaction openly. Meagan had told her a bit about him. He was attractive enough although she didn't always go in for the ponytail look. She knew he and David had played basketball together and he certainly had an athletic build. So he was their flying ace. She thought to herself why not as she told him she'd be happy to accompany him on some outings. She told herself she'd been planning to explore the area anyway and this seemed as good a way as any to do some of that.

Meagan returned inside with Diamond in tow. She and David set about preparing dinner, leaving Mark and Diane to keep track of the puppy and forestall any accidents he might create. The two exchanged pleasantries as they kept an eye on Diamond.

"How long have you practiced law?"

"Nearly four years. I have my own practice in Palm Desert and two other associates with me. I do trials as well as all the other family and individual types of law issues that come up in a rural environment."

"Do you enjoy it?"

"I used to. At first I really thought I was enjoying it but the bloom on the rose has faded a bit. I make a good living at it and that is important to me. But it doesn't excite me and I'm feeling a little antsy."

"What does excite you?"

"I think the interaction with people and knowing I'm helping them. That's the part I like best. And there's some of that to be sure. But most of my time isn't spent that way. Instead I find myself researching, writing, preparing for and trying cases. The personal interaction in a trial is more of a competition than any type of collaboration or personal sharing. I guess I should have known better what it would be like."

"Sometimes it is just as important to find out what we don't like as what we do like. Then we don't have to spend any more time wondering if that's for us."

She looked at him with new respect. That was it exactly. She had been seduced by the chance to make a lot of money and thought it would be fulfilling as well. Maybe now she needed to focus more on what would make her happy.

"Have you ever had a job that made you feel the way you want to feel?"

"In the summers of my undergrad years I interned as a counselor. I minored in psychology because I thought it would provide me good insight for practicing law. I liked helping people realize they could make changes in their life, could take control of it rather than being beaten down by it, and seeing the results of it their attitude and behavior."

"Sounds like you already know what you want to do next."

"Maybe I do. Maybe I just do know." She looked directly at him. She suddenly realized how good he was at listening. Up till now she had done all the talking and he hadn't contributed but a few words. When he had said something it was concise and to the point.

"Have you ever thought about becoming a counselor? You're pretty good at it."

"Me? No, I don't think that's me. I like people well enough but I've always been better with my hands than my head. I like to create or fix things. I've done a lot of building and fixing of things at different times. Then in the Air Force I got to go flying and I was hooked." He looked up and smiled at her. "There's nothing better to me than being up in the sky free as a bird and just taking everything in that's around me. It's as close to heaven as I'm likely to get."

She liked the animation and joy in his face when he talked of flying. Despite his statement to the contrary she thought he had a pretty good handle on people.

But it was clear that flying captured his spirit.

Meagan came in and told them dinner was ready and would they mind adjourning to the dining room. Diane followed Meagan. Mark took Diamond to the mudroom that had been designated as his room while he was learning to control his behavior, and then joined the group at the table.

CHAPTER 45

Most of the talk during dinner revolved around the grand opening events the following day. A ceremonial ribbon cutting at the gate of the B&B at 11:30 am would kick things off. That would be followed by a luncheon in the dining room with additional seating on the deck, weather permitting. After the lunch brief remarks were scheduled from the mayor of Homer, the Homer Chamber of Commerce director, and Carolyn.

Promptly on schedule the following morning, Carolyn used a giant pair of scissors to cut a large purple ribbon strung between the posts at the front gate. Even though representatives from two newspapers were on hand to record the event, Meagan took pictures of everything that transpired. She had decided to make a scrapbook that would serve as a photographic memory of Alaskan Adventures and she wanted to include these moments. David, as was his style, remained in the background and allowed Carolyn to serve as the public face of the organization.

Jerry and the kitchen staff had outdone themselves with the lunch. Everything was homemade from appetizers to entrée's to dessert. The soup that started the meal was made using local razor clams. The salad used local greens, tomatoes and carrots. Salmon and halibut were served in a variety of ways and had been caught the day before. A berry cobbler topped everything off. Several attendees went back for seconds and remarked on the delicious cuisine. The talks were mercifully short and soon the lodge contained only employees and paid guests who were either just taking it easy or had activities scheduled locally in the afternoon. Everyone who attended had received a hat and t-shirt emblazoned with "I Survived Alaskan Adventures" sporting the organizational logo. Paid guests received the same gifts plus a similar sweatshirt.

The real purpose of the grand opening was to kick off the organization operating at maximum capacity. A full complement of staff had been hired, trained and now fulfilled their roles flawlessly. All cabins were occupied and that trend would continue for the next seven weeks. It was only after Labor Day that the rush would drop off. Most of the guests to date had come from word-of-mouth referrals from contacts made by the management team or their friends and relatives. A few had started to trickle in from the website. They were hoping guests would leave favorable evaluations and reviews on travel websites such as Trip Advisor. Meagan was hoping to drive year round guest traffic by tailoring activities and experiences to each season. An example of this was a proposed series of classes and photo shoots of the northern lights during the winter. She hoped to make arrangements for one of the photo shoots to be conducted via dogsled. She was still filling in the details for the slower time from October to April but it was starting to come together.

The small community of Homer had wholeheartedly embraced the program Alaskan Adventures was creating and offering. Local merchants sported flyers in store windows promoting the activities and experience. Some offered discounts off of normal prices for clientele of the B&B. In turn, the organization purchased as much of their supplies locally as possible. Homer thrived on tourism and anything that brought in more visitors would also encourage additional spending. For the most part employees had been hired from the local labor pool further stimulating the economy.

The following day brought the arrival of a couple with two small children. Harold and Patricia Martin lived in the greater Philadelphia area where he was an executive with Sunoco. He had gone to school at Wharton with Carolyn and the two still kept in touch periodically. Carolyn had let him know months ago of the projected opening of the B&B and the Martins had arranged their vacation plans accordingly. The Martins had two children, Robyn was four and Michael was six. Both were towheads with blonde hair and blue eyes. Michael looked like a young version of Harold but it was Robyn who was the apple of her father's eye. Like many proud fathers he carried photos of his family at all times and never hesitated to pull them out and expound. The couple had talked for some time about visiting Alaska and when Carolyn made them aware of what she was doing it seemed like too good an opportunity to pass up. Besides, if he could interest Sunoco in the corporate retreats being offered he could possibly even write the trip off as a business expense. That would make what promised to be a good experience even better in his opinion.

This was Alaskan Adventures' first experience in dealing with the needs of children and some special activities were in the works. Meagan brought Diamond to work with her and the puppy's blue eyes and playful nature quickly fascinated both children. Michael, in particular, was drawn to him and the two became fast friends as they frolicked on the porch outside their cabin. Patricia and the children spent the morning entertained by a young Native American girl who helped them learn about their totems. To his delight Michael found his was the dog. Robyn's turned out to be the deer and Patricia found to her pleasure and surprise hers was the whale. That afternoon they went shopping for souvenir totems in Homer and soon had small wooden figures clutched in their hands. They went to the spit and watched boats unload their catch as eagles and seagulls hovered overhead hoping for their share.

Harold had elected to go fishing for halibut that day and the children were able to see some unloaded so they knew what he would hopefully bring back. Jerry had assured them he would prepare the halibut for their dinner that evening.

When they returned to the B&B the children were met by Jerry who announced it was now time to make cookies. He had located cookie cutters in the shape of their totems and set about showing them how to make the dough and cut it into small deer and dogs. While the cookies baked they helped him prepare appetizers and salads for their dinner. He told them their cookies would be the dessert for the evening. Both were thrilled and brought their mother in to view the results.

At the end of their dinner while the cookies were being served stories were told about deer, dogs and whales. The children went to bed that evening tired but enchanted with the day's activities and what they had learned. Each took their totem figures to bed with them.

CHAPTER 46

The following morning dawned clear and blue. Temperatures were moderate and it promised to be a beautiful day. Mark was scheduled to fly the family and two other guests to Katmai National Park for bear watching. The Otter had been fitted with its pontoons and was now on Beluga Lake near the spit awaiting the arrival of the passengers. David and Meagan would accompany the passengers. David was in the process of obtaining his pilot's license and this trip would add to the hours he was accumulating towards that end. Meagan would continue to record a photographic record of the event for the Alaskan Adventures scrapbook. She would also provide the Martins with copies for their trip memories.

A bear watching excursion is, for many visitors, the highlight of their journey to Alaska. Home to several thousand Alaskan brown bears, Katmai National Park offers perhaps the world's best bear viewing, and certainly the wildest. It is the opportunity of a lifetime to see, observe and photograph numerous grizzlies in their natural habitat. The experience will impress even the most seasoned wilderness traveler, adventurer and photographer.

The flight left Beluga Lake at 9 am for the scenic flight across Cook Inlet. Mark provided a running commentary and orientation as they flew past Cape Douglas, a group of volcanic mountains that protrude into the mouth of Cook Inlet. From the peaks glaciers extended all the way to the beach. They could see beautiful blue-green lakes filled with icebergs. Mark told them that if the water remained calm they would most likely see whales on the return trip. They landed on Katmai's outer coast at the mouth of the Swikshak River. Jerry had prepared a gourmet lunch and they picnicked on the beach there. The vista was spectacular with snow-covered mountains rising 7,000 feet above them to serve as a backdrop.

Because it was early August they headed on towards the northern boundary of the park to Moraine Creek. At this time of year bright red schools of salmon flood into this part of the country and along with their arrival come the bears. The snow-fed rivers are shallow, swift and clear, and the bears feed with a frenzy. They could expect to see literally tens of thousands of spawning red salmon and perhaps twenty bears.

The viewing platform was perched above the river and surrounding shore and afforded amazing views of the activity below. Meagan paused her picture taking to look around. Patricia and Harold had both brought their own cameras and were snapping pictures everywhere. A big male grizzly caught a salmon and was eating it. A sow brought a fish to her two cubs. Michael was standing beside David, his gaze shifting back and forth at the activity, as David explained how the bears were storing fat for the winter. But where was Robyn? She was nowhere to be seen. She put her camera away and began to look around for the little girl.

Robyn had been examining her deer totem when it had fallen to the ground below. She couldn't get to it from the platform so she had gone back along the walkway until she found a spot she could fit through and climb down. She was now walking back along the shoreline below to where she had dropped it. Fortunately no bears had yet noticed the small intruder. Meagan got David's attention and pointed to Robyn. He quickly got the group together and explained what was taking place. He cautioned them to remain silent.

Meagan removed her camera and daypack and set them on the platform. She leaned over and whispered to Robyn trying to get her attention. Meanwhile one of the bear cubs had noticed the girl and, seeing something closer to its own size, was coming to investigate. The second cub soon followed his lead. Robyn was unable to find her totem and sat down and began to cry.

Meagan retreated back down the walkway to a point where she could scale the fence and barricades and get down. She climbed over, lowered herself to the ground, and began to slowly walk back towards Robyn. She didn't know what she was going to do but she knew she had to do something.

The two cubs didn't appear to be aggressive as they approached the little girl, they were mostly curious. They circled her cautiously, sniffing the air. Robyn saw them and smiled, her crying forgotten. She reached out to try and touch one.

As Meagan approached she began speaking quietly to Robyn, trying to keep her calm. She reached her side and the cubs eyed her curiously.

The sow suddenly noticed the absence of her cubs and rose onto two feet searching for them. She saw them with the humans and with a fierce snort she dropped to all fours and moved towards them. All thoughts of salmon were forgotten as she now focused on the need to keep her cubs safe.

Meagan knew the worst thing she could possibly do was to run. The sow would regard her as game and attack long before she could reach the walkway and safety. Even if she didn't have Robyn to contend with she would not be able to escape the bear. She knew the bear wasn't hungry but was only trying to protect her offspring. She couldn't run from it and she certainly couldn't fight it. The bear could kill them both with a single swipe of its paw. What other options did she have?

David continued to keep the group together above the drama unfolding below. He told them to remain silent and motionless so they did not further provoke the mother bear. Patricia and Harold were frozen in fear, their son Michael clutched tightly against them. Patricia's shoulders were shaking as she cried softly.

Another visitor back at the entrance to the walkway had seen what was happening and summoned a park ranger. The ranger retrieved a high-powered rifle and was slowly making his way along the walkway. In the fifty-four year history of the park there had never been a human hurt by bears. He hoped today would not mark the first. And he hoped he would not have to shoot the sow for it would almost certainly condemn the cubs to death as well when winter arrived. David slowly made his way back to the ranger and the two conferred quietly. Grizzlies were notoriously difficult to kill with a single shot, even with a rifle, and they didn't want to risk an injured bear attacking the defenseless woman and little girl.

The bear sprinted towards Meagan, stopped, reared up on its hind legs and roared fiercely. It was enormous as it towered above them. Robyn stared wide-eyed at it as Meagan took her hand and the two stood facing it. The cubs had retreated behind their mother.

Instinct took over as Meagan reached under her shirt and pulled out the pouch containing her talisman and the stone heart. She began softly talking to the bear. "Here now, mother, no one is going to hurt your cubs or you. I, too, am a bear and this is another cub here with me. No one means you or your family harm. I am here at your calling to help you reunite with your salmon lover. Come learn who I am and satisfy yourself. Then return with your family to the river and your feeding." She slowly extended her arm and the pouch towards the bear. The bear lowered itself to all fours and came closer, sniffing cautiously.

The ranger raised the rifle and took aim at the sow. Without saying a word David put his arm out and motioned for him to stop. If he fired now the results could be catastrophic. The gun was slowly lowered and they continued to watch in amazement at the drama unfolding below them.

The bear walked up to Meagan and inhaled the scent of the pouch and its contents. Cocking its head it stared curiously at her as if it knew her and was trying to place her in its memories. Meagan remained motionless with the pouch extended. The bear took another step and breathed in her scent. It licked the hand holding the pouch. Apparently reassured by what she found, she turned and herded her cubs back towards the river and the waiting salmon.

As if in a trance, Meagan picked Robyn up and slowly carried her back towards the walkway. She climbed up the barricade and handed the girl to David. She scrambled back over the fence to the safety of the wooden deck. She looked up at David as if struggling to place him. Then she fainted.

CHAPTER 47

When the bear turned to leave David let out the breath he'd been holding. He hadn't realized he'd been holding it. Without a word he'd walked back to where Meagan was bringing Robyn to safety. When she held the little girl out to him he took her and handed her to the ranger. He took Meagan's hand and helped her back over the railing and barricade onto the walkway. He saw her eyes roll back and caught her as she fell, the pouch still clutched in her hand.

David doubted if he'd ever really understand what had just taken place. He knew the details of it would be forever etched in his mind. He had desperately wanted to go to Meagan's assistance, he would willingly have stood between her and the bear. But a part of him knew that this was something she had to do on her own. And she had done it. And she was alive. That was what mattered.

The Martins were stunned. What they had just seen was beyond their powers of comprehension. When David first brought Robyn's precarious position to their attention they were certain nothing would be able to save her from a mother bear defending her cubs. Then Meagan had appeared beside Robyn and calmly talked to the bear that had apparently understood whatever it was she said. When the bear smelled and then licked her extended hand they were mesmerized. They watched in awe as the bear left with her cubs and Meagan brought Robyn to safety. They could not fathom what their eyes had just seen. They could not believe Meagan had willingly risked her own life to save their daughter by deliberately placing herself in the bear's path. They had never witnessed such an act of heroism before.

For his part, the park ranger was unsure exactly how he was going to complete an incident report on this event. In his twenty-three years of service he had never encountered anything like this. He doubted that anyone who had not seen it firsthand would believe it. He decided he would simply state that a child had managed to get down to the riverbank and had been rescued by another visitor without any problems. No one had been injured and no harm had been done to any wildlife or habitat. That would suffice for the purpose of the report but didn't begin to capture what had actually happened. He still couldn't believe what his eyes had seen.

Meagan awakened to find herself in David's arms as he sat on the walkway. She remembered being with Robyn on the riverbank as the bear approached. She thought she might have reached out her arm to it but from that point on it was all a blur. The next thing she knew she was back on the walkway and David was holding her. She asked about Robyn and found she was with her parents and no harm had come to her. She nodded to show she understood and settled back in his arms without speaking.

It was a subdued group that made its way slowly back to the airplane. Only the two children spoke aloud, the event already dismissed, as they moved on to the next experience. Once they were inside David briefly filled Mark in on what had transpired. They went straight back to Homer without detouring for any further sightseeing.

When they arrived Mark transported the guests back to the B&B. As they returned to their rooms he filled Diane, Carolyn and Jerry in on what had taken place. He said he hadn't seen it himself as he had remained with the plane. He was sure David would have more to say but he had taken Meagan home for now.

David had driven Meagan home and put her to bed. She was exhausted and he couldn't blame her. She fell almost immediately into a deep sleep. He lay beside her on the bed, stroking her head, as she slept. He watched and thought about what had happened, what he had felt, what could have been. He did not ever want to go through that kind of fear again, a fear of losing her forever. It had shaken him to the core. He couldn't imagine life without her. After watching and holding her for an hour he joined her in bed and fell asleep.

CHAPTER 48

Meagan awakened to find David snuggled up against her. She stroked his face and his eyes opened. She pulled his head to hers and kissed him deeply. What began as a gentle kiss suddenly turned fierce as he pulled her to him roughly. He crushed her to him, as if trying to possess her completely. His mouth roamed her face, her neck, her shoulders. His hands found her breast and he squeezed it, placing it in his mouth and sucking hungrily. She could feel his complete lack of control and it excited her.

He rolled her to her back, parted her legs, and mounted her. All pretense of tenderness was gone as he pounded himself into her again and again. She arched to meet him caught up in the heat of the moment. With a great effort he raised his head and looked at her.

"I'm not trying to hurt you, Meagan. I don't want to hurt you. I just need to have you. I have to have you now."

"You're not hurting me, David. I'm not fragile and I won't break. Don't stop now. Whatever you do don't stop now."

He abandoned any restraints and continued to plunge into her. His pace picked up and his body was coated with sweat. She could feel his peak coming and she answered it with a frenzy of her own. She felt his shudders as he emptied himself into her and cried her name aloud. She dug her nails into his buttocks as she pulled him deeper inside. She tightened her muscles around him as her own climax overtook her and she succumbed to the sensation.

CHAPTER 49

Meagan stayed home from work the next day and Diane kept her company. She shared what she remembered of the encounter with the bear. David had previously told Diane what he had observed, and the helplessness he had felt. She sensed he was running close to the edge of his emotions at the present and it all revolved around his deep feelings for Meagan.

The music was playing softly and Diane was immersed in a book. Meagan had her laptop out and was downloading pictures from her camera. She hadn't done this in some time and she needed to get it all organized and the memory card cleared.

As she worked her way through the pictures she came across the ones taken the day of her flight with Mark to Nanwalek. Most of them were okay, she had some nice landscapes, a good shot of a pelican on the spit, and some good ones of the shops. But one particular close-up shot of the young man gazing at the ocean stopped her in her tracks.

He couldn't have been more than a teenager yet he looked as if he had the weight of the world on his shoulders. His shoulders sagged and his face looked exhausted. She wondered what set of circumstances had combined to make a person so young feel as if the world was against him. She had managed to capture the sorrow and suffering of a teenager utterly without hope, waiting, fearing what the next day would bring. The image somehow managed to transfer the emotions he felt to the person viewing the photograph.

She made a copy of the file and brought it into PhotoShop Elements on her laptop. It didn't require much manipulation or correction. She made a few adjustments to the contrast to highlight the features on his face. She saved it and printed it on photo paper. She took it and several others she had printed in the living room to show Diane.

"This one of the young man is absolutely incredible, Meagan. As I look at it I can feel his fear, his desperation, and his hopelessness. Your picture makes the viewer experience the same emotions. It's a remarkable shot."

That evening Carolyn and Jerry came over for dinner to join the four people staying at David's house. They had wanted to see for themselves that Meagan was okay and they relayed the Martin's gratitude for what she had done.

As they sat around the table with a glass of wine in hand Diane passed the photos Meagan had printed out around. There were a lot of comments about the one of the young man. David, in particular, stared at it for a long time before finally passing it on.

After dinner they were all sitting on pillows around the fireplace. Diane had noticed David's earlier strong reaction to the picture Meagan had taken of the young man. She asked him to share with them what he thought the young man was feeling.

David looked again at the picture and answered without really thinking, "He's about 18 years old and he's confused and frightened."

He began talking from the standpoint of the boy but soon switched and began telling it from his point of view. He was sitting down rocking back and forth with his hands over his face and he was crying. He continued to cry with great racking sobs and Diane moved in to sit beside him and asked what was going on inside of him.

"I just want to be loved. All I've ever wanted is

someone to love me. I want someone to care about me unconditionally so I can be who I am. When will someone love me? When can I relax and be real? When can I just be me? What have I done that's so bad? I'm so tired of hurting others and being hurt. I can't stand it any more. Please just love me. I'm so tired, so very, very tired.

The words poured out of his mouth as if a cap had blown off when the pressure became too great. Tears poured from his eyes and his nose ran profusely. At times he could hardly get the words out between the sobs.

"Who are you David?" asked Diane softly.

"I'm me, now. I'm me as a child. I'm me as a teenager. I'm me at all the different times in my life. It's always the same, the feelings are always the same. No one really loves me, no one really cares. I try so hard. God, I try so hard. No one knows how hard I try but it never works out. I always end up alone, with no one caring about me. Will I ever be happy? Will I ever be loved? When will it all end? God, how I want all this pain to end! I'm so tired of starting over. New people. New relationships. Won't somebody please just love me for who I am?"

"Who are you, David."

"I don't know. I've been searching all my life for

who I am. I've been looking for the real David. If I find the real David I'm sure someone will love him. But I don't even know how I'll know if and when I find him. I don't know if he exists. Sometimes I'm afraid there isn't anything to me. I feel like a chameleon, all I ever do is color myself to adapt to my environment. I'm so adaptable. I can be anything anyone ever wants me to be in order to get what I need. But nobody knows the real me. No one knows who I really am. I want someone to know me as I am and still love me. No one ever has. No one ever will."

"Will you tell the people here that you've been fooling them, David? Will you tell Carolyn and Jerry and Mark and Meagan that you've been fooling them?" asked Diane.

"That's not it exactly. It's not that I'm fooling then, it's just that they don't know who I really am. They only know pieces of me and I want someone to know all of me and still love me and care about me. I'm so tired of being what others want me to be. And I'm so good at it."

David continued to cry in great, wracking painful sobs. Between them he tearfully and painfully told everyone his story of how he'd never felt loved. He'd looked for relationships but it always ended up the same, he'd end up leaving the other person, he'd end up rejecting them before they would have the chance to reject him. That's the way it had always been and how it always worked out. At times he was 28, at times he was 18, at times he was 8 years old. The feeling was always the same. No one really loves him. No one really cares. He experienced all the ages he'd lived through and it was constant, the feeling was always constant. David was unlovable.

"On the surface everyone sees me as a very nice, successful and capable person. But they don't know the real me. If they knew who I really am they wouldn't like me. Every time anyone told me what a good job I'd done or what a nice person I am, internally I'd say yes, but if you only knew."

"If they only knew what, David?"

"If they only knew that at the heart of me there's a black spot. There's a great big huge piece of blackness at the very center of me. And I have to keep everyone from ever getting close to it. If they ever get close to it I know something terrible will happen – they will unconditionally reject me. The pain of rejection to date has already been as much as I can bear. How then can I ever let somebody in to the very center of me where they can see this blackness? I can't take the risk of letting someone know the real me and then reject me. That would be more than I can bear. That would surely kill me."

"What is this black spot, David?"

"I don't know. I've puzzled over that question more times than I could ever tell you. I've examined it as a child, a teenager, and as an adult. It's always the same. Right there at the very center of David is a black box. I know that at all costs I must keep everyone away from it. I've wondered if it contains some hideous flaw, some horrible defect in my make-up. I can't conceive of anything I've ever done that is so wrong that it must be hidden in this manner. I've also entertained the idea there may be nothing inside, that at the very core of me there's a void. That spot is an intense place to be, I know that. When I begin getting near it the air is charged with electricity. The idea of a void existing there scares me worse than the idea of a flaw. If there's a void it means I'm just a worthless person, there's nothing to me. The essence of David is nothingness."

He reached a point where he could seem to go no further. He was stuck. He was exhausted. But he wanted to go on. He knew he couldn't stop now. The pain of it was getting more and more intense. Suddenly he could no longer tell it from the standpoint of David and he began recounting the story of Peer Gynt.

"I've heard the story of Peer Gynt. He was a person who journeyed through life looking for the real Peer Gynt. He tried many trades and experienced many diverse experiences in his quest to find out who he

really was. At the end of the play, in a soliloquy to the
audience, he is peeling an onion away layer by layer,
looking for the essence of the onion. As he peels away
the last layer he discovers that the onion was, in fact,
made up of all those layers and that there is nothing
more. He suddenly realizes that Peer Gynt is a
composite of all these roles."

"I heard this story in my late teens and it frightened
me. Somehow I want there to be more to David than
all these roles. I want there to be an essence to David
above and beyond these roles."

David could go no further and sat there waiting for
something to happen. He felt he'd given Diane a key of
some sort but he didn't know what it unlocked. Diane
moved next to David and placed her hand on his
shoulder and said, "I'm holding the onion that is David
in my hand now and I'm peeling away the top layer.
What is it?"

"It's me trying to maintain a relationship with
Meagan. Trying to get her to love me, trying
desperately to hold everything together."

"And the next layer as I peel away the layers of the
onion that is David?"

"That's me trying to build Alaskan Experiences.
I'm trying to build something that will help people just
relax and enjoy the world."

Somehow David was aware that all the layers consisted of roles or relationships, that these were the things that held the key to his validation.

"I'm at the last layer of David's onion and I'm peeling it away. What's there?"

A startled shout came from David as he concentrated and visualized the removal of the layer. Sitting in the middle of the "onion" and smiling broadly was a small child, clad only in diapers, that he knew was him.

Diane asked David to go back and be that little child. David sat there on the floor by the fireplace and gradually went back inside the little child who he now knew was Davey. It was a strange and eerie feeling because there were multiple levels of him functioning simultaneously. There was the thirty-one year-old adult David sitting by the fireplace recounting the story. There was another part of him that became the little child and experienced all the feelings of him and saw it through his eyes. And there was a third part of him perched up near the ceiling, above both David and Davey, silently observing everything. This part of him was like a recorder and missed nothing.

He began crying again.

"All I want is to be loved. Please, all I want is to be loved. Why won't somebody love me? What have I done? I'll be good. Oh God, I'll be so good. Please love me. Won't you please love me?"

"Who do you want to love you, David?"

"Mommy. I want my Mommy. I want my Mommy to love me and she doesn't. My Mommy doesn't love me and I want her to so badly. Please love me Mommy. Please, please, please, please. I'll do whatever you want. Just love me. Just care about me. Please."

He lay down and curled up and cried and cried, periodically calling out for his Mommy. She never came and he continued to cry. He shifted back and forth between the David telling this tale and the little Davey on the ground. At one point he told of how he'd made a successful break from his Mom. He'd moved in with his Dad, became a basketball star, even started a business and became wealthy. He had proved he could take care of his own needs.

"Oh, you fooled her too," said Diane.

It was like he'd been hit with a sledgehammer. That's exactly what he'd done! He'd fooled her, too! He'd fooled himself, too. He never had made the break. He still needed her to want him and care about him and love him and he'd spent his whole life trying to prove he didn't want or need that. And the harder he tried the more he proved the opposite. He cried anew.

As he was back being Davey and crying for Mommy again, Diane asked him if he would tell Mommy how he felt. She sat a chair in front of him, to hold Mommy, and had David ask her a question, then get into the chair and answer it for her.

"Why don't you love me, Mommy?"

"I'm trying to get my own needs met, David, and be able to survive myself."

"Then why do you always remove someone when I start to get close to them and to love them?"

"Because if I can't love you and be what you need, I can't let anyone else love you either and take my role. Somehow that pushes me down even further."

"Then what am I supposed to do? Am I supposed to die? Don't you realize you're killing me? Don't you care? YOU'RE KILLING ME AND YOU DON'T EVEN CARE! YOU'RE KILLING ME AND I HAVEN'T DONE ANYTHING WRONG! WHAT AM I SUPPOSED TO DO?"

There was nothing but silence.

David became angrier than he'd ever been. He began shaking violently as he sobbed and cried out to his Mommy in anger and frustration.

"Get out of my life! If you won't love me then get

out of my life! Leave me alone. LEAVE ME ALONE!
At least allow me to find someone to love me for
myself. Please don't take them away any more. I can't
stand it. I CAN'T STAND IT!"

Diane went behind David and sat on his shoulders
as he sat on the ground. He was crying and shaking.
She said, "I'm never going to leave you alone. You'll
have to kill me to get rid of me. I'll never let you alone.
I'll always hold you back. I'll always push you down.
You'll have to kill me."

David sat bent over, holding a pillow, crying
violently. He had never been so angry before in his life.
He began shouting again.

"Leave me alone! Get out of my life! Why don't
you die? Why won't you just go away and die? Leave
me alone! GET OUT OF MY LIFE! GO AWAY
AND DIE!"

He looked up at Diane as he held the pillow in his
hands. He thought all he had to do was move his hands
apart and the pillow would rip into pieces. He was
shaking violently and couldn't control it. Diane took
the pillow and placed it on the chair telling him it was
his mother.

"Go ahead and kill her," she said. "It's the only way
you'll ever get rid of her. Kill her!"

David wanted to do it so badly. His muscles were killing him as he sat bent over facing the chair. He continued to shake as he cried. For some reason he couldn't bring himself to hit her, to kill her. He cried more and became angrier. Finally, he spoke.

"I won't kill my mother to save myself. I can't do it. I won't do it."

"What other alternative do you have, David?"

"To go inside my black spot and see what it is all about."

"Do you want to go there?"

"I've always wanted to go there."

He sat on the floor trying to relax. His muscles were so tense that he couldn't just let them loose. He ended up relaxing in jerks, like undergoing a seizure. At last he was somewhat less tense and sat there on the floor.

"Do you know how to get in to your black spot?" Diane asked.

"Oh yes, I know how to get in there. There's a whirlpool on one end and all I have to do is step off into it. It will take me there. I've been to the brink of it many times before in my life. I never thought I would dare enter, though."

Up till this point he'd taken a number of risks with this group of people. He'd let them see parts of him that no one else had ever seen, not even himself. As he stood on the brink of the whirlpool he was aware that from here on the risk was entirely his. If he found what he thought might exist inside that blackness he would probably kill himself. Who can exist when they know for a certainty that their essence is nothing? The risk was all David's now.

He stepped in. He immediately lost his balance as he began spinning around and he fell over on the floor despite the fact he'd been sitting down. He began describing aloud to the rest of the people around him what he was experiencing.

"I'm spinning round and round and being pulled downward. I'm up to my armpits in the blackness with my arms, head and shoulders out of it. I can see the light up above me growing smaller as I'm being carried down. The light is continuing to fade and I'm carried around a twist in the whirlpool and I can no longer see the entrance. Somehow I can see in here although everything around me is black. It's like going through a tunnel that is winding, twisting and silently rotating. I am being carried around numerous twists and bends like a twig on water. I'm almost there. I know as soon as I go around the next bend I'll be at the very core of my existence. I'll be at the heart of me. I'm anxious and apprehensive because I know I will soon confront my essence. I know if I want to, if I make a supreme effort, I can remove myself from this inky river and go back the way I came. I also know that if I do, I will never again return to this place."

"Do you want to continue?" asks Diane.

"I have to. I can't go back now. I've come too far. But I'm scared. I'm terrified."

He continued to drift on toward the final corner. As he neared it he could see light coming from around it. As he drifted around the corner he screamed.

Diane asked him what was there and he said he'd share in a moment but he first needed some time to experience and comprehend this himself. After a few moments he continued.

"The tunnel has widened into a room and there in the middle of it, lying on his stomach on a white blanket, surrounded by light, is a little baby. He's about six months old and has no clothes on. I know he's me and his name is Davey. I'm walking over to him. Now I'm picking him up and holding him in my arms."

David and Davey both began to cry. The tears this time are ones of happiness and joy, celebrating their reunion.

David suddenly realized that for thirty-one years he'd carried this box around thinking there was something hideous inside. He'd always thought that the box was constructed to keep something locked inside. In reality it was constructed to keep everything in the world out. There was nothing wrong with him. There's just a part of him that was so fragile, so tender and so vulnerable that he built a fortress for it to keep it safe, to keep it alive. And that fortress was so necessary and so impregnable that he couldn't even allow himself to penetrate it for the last thirty-one years. He wasn't keeping anything about himself from hurting anyone, he was keeping part of him from being hurt any more.

As David was lying on the floor, exhausted, Diane suggested that he not throw the black box away just yet. She said he had put a lot of energy into constructing and maintaining it and that energy could now be rechanneled into other things.

David continued to lie on the pillows. He couldn't remember ever being so emotionally and physically drained. As he was lying there, surrounded by people he'd known for varying lengths of time, he was suddenly conscious of the fact that this was the first time in his life he could ever remember being with people and not having a role to play, a facade to maintain.

CHAPTER 50

Meagan was overwhelmed. She had just watched the man she loved go through the most intense emotional experience she had ever witnessed. She had been caught up in his pain, and her own, as had everyone in the room. Everyone could relate to his doubts and his fears because it touched a similar spot and feeling in each of them. She marveled at the power of the mind and the control it could exert over our behavior. She knew this was a turning point in David's life and wondered what would happen next.

Diane came and sat beside her. She took Meagan's hand in hers and they sat there quietly as David was relaxing and regaining his composure.

"You realize the reason he put himself through that experience is because of you. He is so fearful of repeating the cycle of past failed relationships and he wants so badly for what the two of you share to succeed that he finally had to go inside and confront his demons. It was the only way he could move forward. It took extraordinary strength and determination to do it. In my experience it is rare that someone shows that kind of courage. He's going to need your love and understanding now more than ever."

Meagan went over and sat beside David. She put his head in her lap and ran her hands through his hair. She thought about how quickly he had come to mean so much to her as tears streamed down her cheeks.

"I love you so very much, my David. I'm not your mother and I can't give you what she never gave to you. But I can give you all the love I have within me and I will. My heart and soul belong to you."

David continued to lie in her lap. He opened his eyes and gazed up at her. He, too, had tears running down his cheeks as he said, "I love you, Meagan. I have from the start. I've known it for a long time but I didn't know how to tell you or what kept me from saying it before. Now I know and I have no reason to fear telling you. So I will. I love you. I guess you're going to have to get used to hearing it. I've been holding it inside of me for a long time and now it's finally free."

Carolyn and Jerry got up and said their goodbyes. Diane and Mark walked outside to watch the late evening sunset colors. David was still exhausted. Meagan and he walked to their bedroom and climbed into bed where she held him until he fell asleep. She continued to hold him a long time afterwards thinking. She had been waiting for him to tell her he loved her, to be able to finally express it aloud. And he had. Now their relationship could move forward free of any restraints. Finally she, too, fell asleep.

CHAPTER 51

The two sat comfortably side-by-side in the swing on the porch watching the sunset's fireworks creep across the sky. It was cool but not cold and they were each lost in their own thoughts. After several minutes had passed Mark turned to her.

"That was a powerful experience for me in that room. I think I was just as caught up in it at times as David."

"I believe we all harbor those same kinds of fears and doubts. We get hurt, maybe not even knowing we have, and figure out how to make the pain go away, even if it means denying it exists. I guess it is an innate part of our means of survival."

"I was really impressed with what you did. You seemed to know just what to say to help him keep moving forward until he could get it all out."

"He himself kept giving me the clues as to where he wanted to go next. I just had to give them back to him and nudge him a bit."

"You did an astounding job of it. Thank you for doing that for him. He's someone I care about a lot. He was stuck and couldn't figure out how to get unstuck. He's done so much already in life despite the baggage he carried. I wonder what will come next."

"If I'm any judge of things it will involve Meagan."

"That it will. That it will." He paused for a moment before continuing. "You know, you yourself came to life in there. You positively glowed while you helped him on his journey. You might want to consider counseling and helping others as a career. If not that, at least doing some volunteer work. You're a natural at it."

She let that sink in. She was good at it. She had just proved she was good at it. And she liked how she felt when she was able to help someone remove obstacles from their life and move forward. Now if she could just figure out how to apply that to her own as well.

CHAPTER 52

When David opened his eyes the next morning he saw Meagan sleeping peacefully beside him. Her long brown hair lay in careless disarray on the pillow. He watched her slow and even breathing. The events of the previous evening were vivid in his mind. How could he have misinterpreted things for such a long time? He was going to have to go back inside at some point and let little Davey come out and grow up. Now he would be able to help him with that he thought, he could do more than just keep him from being hurt. An image of his mother popped into his mind. He thought he might better understand her now. She, too, had been hurt and struggled to protect herself. He didn't think she had deliberately tried to hurt him and she probably didn't even know she had. The last time they spoke it was in anger and he had resolved never to talk with her again. He was going to have to break that resolve at some point. He owed it to her and himself.

For now he was going to enjoy the sensation of knowing he could love Meagan and tell her that. It was a heady feeling and he realized a lot of barriers had been removed from having the kind of relationship he'd always wanted to have with a woman. He felt like he might be able to take on anything now and succeed. It was the first time he'd ever felt like that about a relationship. He knew he could do it with a business. Now he could be successful in what might be the most important aspect of his life. His future was his to create. And he planned to do just that.

He pulled Meagan against him slowly so as to not disturb her. She sleepily murmured his name without really waking. He relished the feeling of closeness he experienced being with her. She told him his arms provided her with a sheltered spot where she felt safe and secure. He felt the same way when he was intertwined with her. The world was held at bay and the only thing real at this moment was the two of them. She knew everything about him now. He had laid bare his most inner self before her. She hadn't recoiled or run. Instead she had said she would give him everything she had to give. What a lucky man he was to have her in his life.

So what was next? Did he want to get married? Did he want to have a family? He had always thought he would never marry, never have children. He understood now that it was not just him he had been protecting. He had not wanted to ever be in a position to hurt anyone else as badly as he had hurt. So he had not allowed himself to get close enough to either be hurt or hurt another. With what he now knew he might have to reconsider those decisions because the reasons he'd made them were no longer valid. He fell back asleep with Meagan still in his arms.

CHAPTER 53

All too soon the week had passed and Diane returned to Southern California. Meagan had been involved in pulling together more ideas for increasing off-season traffic so Mark had flown her back to Anchorage to connect with her flight to the "lower 48". David was bursting with energy. The B&B was full and Alaskan Adventures was humming. It felt good. He felt good.

The Martins had returned to Philadelphia five days earlier. Tears had flowed freely when they said their goodbyes to Meagan and they thanked her profusely for what she had done for their daughter and their family. Robyn hugged and kissed her and gave her a drawing of the mother bear and cubs she had made. It was proudly displayed in Meagan's office.

Word of Meagan's heroism had spread quickly throughout Homer. Children were highly valued and cherished in the fabric of rural life and she found herself immediately accepted by the local community. When she had tried to pay for her muffins at the bakery that morning they had refused it telling her it was their way of thanking her for what she had done for the Martins. An unspoken fact was how badly the death of a small child would have impacted tourism and the local economy. While uncomfortable with the attention she was grateful for the acceptance she felt. She had never felt she belonged in San Diego, never really felt like she was part of anything. It had just been someplace she was while she pursued the goal of making money. Here she was part of something greater than herself. She liked that. A lot.

True to his word, Harold had given them an entrée to Sunoco. Carolyn had received a call from the Director of Human Resources asking about tailoring some retreats to the needs of their executives and senior management. She and Meagan were preparing a proposal in response to their request. Both were excited and ideas were being churned out rapidly. A phone call for Meagan interrupted their work. She noticed it was a Dallas, Texas area code but didn't recognize the number. She put it on the speakerphone.

"Miss Turner, thank you for taking my call. I realize you don't know me but my name is Richard

Martin and I am Harold Martin's father. He called me after they got back from Alaska and told me what you did for Robyn. I wanted to call and extend my personal thanks as our granddaughter is very, very important to my wife and me. I am so grateful to you for your saving her life."

She looked at Carolyn. She could hear the heartfelt emotion in his voice.

"Mr. Martin I very much appreciate your call. I cannot tell you how glad I am for how things turned out as well. Robyn is a delightful young girl and I'm happy I was there and able to help. I still don't know exactly what happened and how but it did."

"Yes, Harold and Patricia were a little astonished as well about what took place." He paused a moment and then continued. "My wife Barbara and I have talked of little else for the past couple of days. I'm due to retire soon and hope to be able to spend a lot of the time I'll have available then with our grandchildren. You've enabled that hope to remain alive. We are taking the liberty of sending something to you. You should be receiving it tomorrow. I hope you will accept it in the spirit in which it's being given."

"Mr. Martin, I…"

"Please call me Richard. I feel as if you're part of our family now."

"Then please call me Meagan. Richard, it isn't necessary to give me anything. I simply did it to help Robyn and because I was in a position to do it."

"Yes, I know that. It is because you were so concerned about Robyn and unconcerned about your own safety that we decided to do what we did. Please just accept it with our gratitude. I hope we have the opportunity to meet in person at some point in the near future. Goodbye, Meagan, and please know you have my and Barbara's eternal gratitude."

The call was disconnected. Meagan and Carolyn looked at each other for a moment and then returned to the proposal and their ideas.

The following day as Meagan was working in her office there was a knock on her door. David and Carolyn brought in an enormous bouquet of red roses, a small white box, and an envelope and placed them on the table. A courier had just delivered them. Meagan inhaled the scent of the roses. They were beautiful and smelled so good. A card on the box said simply "To keep Robyn and Michael in your mind." She opened the box and found Baccarat crystal figurines of a deer and a dog. She smiled knowing they represented the children's totems and placed them in her window where they would reflect the sunlight in a rainbow of colors throughout her office.

When she opened the envelope she found a letter and another envelope. She read the letter.

"Dear Meagan,

There is nothing in this world as important as our family to us. Without them nothing has the same value. If you don't already realize that in your life we are sure you will at some point in the future.

Please accept the enclosed gift from us as but a small token of our appreciation.

This gift is given freely and we place you under no obligation save one. If you ever find yourself in a position where you have the ability to help another person who needs it and you have the means please do it without reservation. You will find out how much you gain by giving.

We hope you will use this to do something that brings as much happiness into your life as you have brought into ours.

With much love from both of us,

Richard and Barbara Martin."

Meagan opened the envelope. It contained a check made out to her from the Richard and Barbara Martin Trust Account. The amount was for fifty thousand dollars.

Astonished, she leaned back in her chair. Without a word she handed the letter to David and Carolyn. When they had read it she handed them the check.

"What a thoughtful gesture," exclaimed Carolyn. "What are you going to do with it?"

"I have no idea. I really have no idea at the moment. I'll let you know when I do."

CHAPTER 54

Meagan called Patricia Martin at her home in Philadelphia. She shared with her what Harold's parents had done. Patricia said they had already shared their plans with her and Harold. She told her that Richard lived in Dallas and was the chairman of AT&T. He was retiring next year after a lengthy and highly successful career in the telecom field. He was a self-made billionaire who believed in giving back to others. Before they hung up she again thanked Meagan for what she had done.

That afternoon Meagan went for a walk along the beach and out onto the spit. When she had worked at McLary & Burns she had wanted to accumulate money for all the things she could buy, where she could travel, what she could have. Somehow they no longer seemed of such paramount importance. Between the selling of her condo, her savings and her retirement accounts she had nearly $350,000 put aside. She could live comfortably and still add to that just on what she made from her job. By most people's standards she was already well off. So then, what did she want to do with this unexpected gift?

She thought back to her own upbringing. She had been raised in a loving home that valued family above all else, just like the sentiments espoused by Richard and Barbara. While they had not been wealthy money-wise they had been rich in the love that filled the household. Even when times were lean they had been happy and even managed to give some back to the community in which they lived.

As she walked out on the spit she came to where she had taken the picture of the young man that had so profoundly affected David. An idea struck her and she returned home to get a copy of the picture. Returning to the spit she walked among the businesses and asked people if they knew the identity of the young man. She finally found a person working at the fish packing facility who told her what she wanted to know.

After dinner that evening she was sitting with David in the living room. Music was playing softly and a fire was going.

"You're quiet tonight."

"I've been thinking a lot about what Richard and Barbara did and what I want to do."

"And have you reached a conclusion?"

"Yes. I have.   You know, when I was going to school my goal was to get enough money to be able to do things like fly to Paris and sip wine on the Champs-Elysees and buy nice things to wear."

"And now?"

"Now that doesn't even enter into the equation.   It seems so trite and meaningless.   How did you decide what to do with your money after you made it?   You must have had dreams you could now decide to fulfill."

"I did.   I must admit I did travel and bum around and do some of the things you mention.   I suppose it was fun for a while.   But like you say, it didn't mean anything.   I had to find something that was important, something I could sink my teeth into.   I think first I had to find myself.   Along the way I found Alaska.   At least that provided me with an environment that let me think about the other things.   I was able to relax enough to think about what really mattered.   I wanted to be able to recreate that feeling for others."

"I think I understand.   And, David?"

"Yes?"

"I found out who that person was in the picture I took down on the spit. His name is Henry and he's from Nanwalek although now he's going to school here in Homer at the college. I have his contact info. I want to meet him and talk with him. Somehow it must be important for us to meet. Would you like to join me to do that?"

"I'd like that very much."

"I'll get in touch with him and see when we can set something up."

CHAPTER 55

At noon the next day Henry Corniloff arrived at the B&B to meet with Meagan and David. He had been intrigued with Meagan's call and had some free time so out of curiosity came to satisfy it. Meagan showed him the picture and told him when she had taken it. He examined it with interest.

Henry told her that his family lived in the village of Nanwalek. He was staying in Homer while attending Kenai Peninsula College. His family didn't have a lot of money and he was putting himself through school working at Coal Point Seafoods on the spit helping process fishermen's catches. He had been working that day and had just found out a friend of his who went to high school with him had committed suicide the night before. Even though they were both underage they had gone out and shared a few beers the previous evening.

He hadn't had any idea his friend was going to do this. He had returned to his apartment about 11 pm because he knew he had to work the next day. When his friend hadn't shown up for work someone went by his place and found him. He shot himself. There was no note. When he found out he went out on his break and sat there wondering if there was something he could have done or should have done. He just didn't know. It was such a waste. There could have, no make that should have, been so much ahead of him. The two of them had grown up together in Nanwalek. They both had had dreams. He realized these things happened but this was the first time it had hit so close to home for him. He had just been sitting there wondering about what it all meant when Meagan had taken the picture. He handed it back to her.

As she took it she asked what he was studying. It was fisheries management. The people in his village lived a sustenance lifestyle and he wanted to be able to contribute to their future. She thanked him for coming by and for sharing. She told him how sorry she was about his friend and assured him it had not been his fault. He said he knew that but still wondered if there hadn't been something he might have done.

As he was walking out the door Meagan stopped him with a question. "Henry, what was your friend's name?"

"It was Larry. Larry Ivanov. He would have been nineteen next month."

Henry left. David excused himself saying he had a few things requiring his attention as well. Left alone Meagan sat and thought for a long time.

CHAPTER 56

They were lying in bed that night when she turned to David and told him what she wanted to do with the money. She would use half of it to set up a scholarship at the college in the name of Larry Ivanov. That half would go to Henry so he could continue his schooling with less worry. With the other half she wanted to go to Nanwalek and see if something could be done to proactively reach out to young people to give them hope for the future. She wanted to reach them before the despair overtook them that would cause them to contemplate suicide. There must be some organization there, perhaps a church or a tribal office, which would be willing to undertake this. It wasn't a lot of money but it would at least be a start.

"So what do you think?"

"It's an excellent idea and certainly something that is needed. How can I help?"

"You already have. You've given me belief in myself, in my capability to do things I didn't know I could do before. I'm sure there will be many ways you will help as I move forward."

It was a while before she finally fell asleep as her mind kept mulling over the next steps and how best to take them.

The next afternoon she went to Kenai Peninsula College and located the Financial Assistance Office. She told the person at the desk what she wanted to do and soon found herself in the office of the Director of Financial Assistance. She was assured that she could indeed make an endowment in the name of Larry Ivanov and earmark it for Henry Corniloff's use. She said she hoped to add to it at some point in time and make it an ongoing scholarship but she would start with this. She asked that this be kept between them for the present until she was ready to let the recipient know.

After doing a little research on the internet she had determined that the residents of Nanwalek were primarily from the Chugach native peoples of Alaska. A non-profit organization named Chugachmiut had been formed in 1974 to administer to the overall economic, social and cultural needs of the people of the

Chugach Region.   Their administrative office was located in Anchorage. She called them and learned that the Vice Chair of the Board of Directors was from Nanwalek. She called the Vice Chair and explained what she wanted to do. When she said she wanted to do it in the name of Larry Ivanov she both felt and heard the emotion in the man's voice. He told Meagan his sister was Larry's mother. Something inside her clicked as yet another piece of the puzzle fell into place. She told him of the scholarship she was also setting up and how she hoped this would be just the beginning of something that would continue to grow.

That night she shared with David the process she had put in motion. As he held her in his arms he told her what a special person she was and how fortunate he felt that she had come into his life. Relaxed and content with all she had begun she fell asleep quickly.

CHAPTER 57

She awoke to find David cuddling against her. Kissing the back of her neck he murmured, "Good morning, Meagan. I love you."

Turning toward him she replied, "Good morning, David. I love you, too."

It had become a ritual with them and she liked it. The last thing they said to each other before falling asleep at night and the first in the morning upon awakening was to tell each other of their love. It was a little thing but it was such a good way to both begin and end the day. It insured there were no ill feelings or unfinished business between them and reaffirmed their commitment to each other. And it gave her renewed and positive energy with which to tackle the day's tasks.

"What's on your agenda for today?"

"I need to head up towards Anchorage this afternoon. Planning to leave about 3. Are you up for a drive?"

She thought about it. She was tied up this morning preparing some reports and getting caught up on the accounting. But she could certainly be ready to go by then.

"Sounds good to me. What's the dress code?"

"We're good as we are. Nothing formal required. Since it's Friday we can come in late tomorrow if we want. So we don't have to worry if we're out late. I'll meet you home about 2:30 or so."

With a lot to do the time passed quickly. She had always found it was much easier to work time to death than to try and kill it. She finished the month end financial reports she'd be presenting to the management group on Monday and emailed everyone their own copy to review beforehand. There were no surprises and they were a little ahead on projected income and just about even on expenses to date. There shouldn't be a lot of questions or issues.

She arrived home at the appointed hour. David had gotten their small suitcases out and was packing for an overnight stay. He said it was just in case it got late and they decided not to drive all the way back. She obligingly assembled her toiletries and a change of clothes. She left a note for Mark about tending to Diamond's needs. She had already taken him outside for a walk and a potty break.

The ride up the Seward Highway was always pleasant. Even though she had made the drive a number of times the scenery was always a little different. The weather was partly cloudy and the temperature moderate. She smiled as they passed the Kenai Princess Lodge and again when the turnoff to Hope appeared. Soon they passed the turnoff to Seward and were headed along Turnagain Arm toward Anchorage.

She glanced questioningly at David when he turned off at Girdwood. The sign had said Alyeska Resort. She knew this was where Carolyn and Jerry had been working when David first met them.

"Just thought we'd take a little detour. There is something I want to show you."

The chateau-style hotel was breathtaking. Nestled in a lush valley the resort was surrounded by mountain peaks and hanging glaciers. David found a parking space and they went inside. It was a perfect blend of modern amenities and rich Native touches that managed to bring the majestic beauty of Alaska's great outdoors inside. David walked to the desk and spoke to the person on duty. After receiving a nod he returned to Meagan's side.

"Let's get our coats. We're taking a tram ride."

They returned to the car and retrieved their jackets. They walked to the tram entrance and boarded. Soon they were on their way up the hill. Meagan looked around wide-eyed as they ascended 2,300 feet up the mountain. They exited the tram and followed the pathway to the Seven Glaciers Restaurant. They were quickly ushered inside and seated at a table next to a window providing a panoramic view of the mountains, glaciers and even the ocean beyond. A bottle of Conundrum arrived at the table.

"David, what's going on?"

"It's our three month anniversary. Don't tell me you've already forgotten?"

She chuckled at the thought he'd remember monthly anniversaries for them. He had gotten her Diamond for their first month's anniversary. The second hadn't produced any type of celebration she could recall. Why then this for the third? She decided not to worry about it and instead proceeded to simply enjoy the experience. They selected the Chef's Prix Fixe menu. An appetizer of Alaskan king crab cakes was followed by a scallop bisque soup and then a baby greens salad with lemon tarragon dressing. Their entrée was pan-roasted Alaskan halibut with smoked eggplant, warm squash salad, ricotta dumplings and tomato vinaigrette. A decadent chocolate cake that was closer to fudge than cake completed the meal. They finished their wine and rose to leave.

"Thank you, David. What a wonderful surprise. I had no idea anything this magnificent existed here."

"It is a beautiful setting isn't it?" He led the way to a small bench. "Please sit down, Meagan." She obliged and looked up at him. She took a deep breath when he retrieved a small box from his pocket and knelt before her.

"Meagan, since the moment we met you are never out of my thoughts. You bring a joy and fulfillment to my life that I didn't know it was possible to experience. Because of you I broke through lifelong barriers and learned how to love. I don't want to ever lose what we share. I want to spend the rest of my life with you. I want to explore the world with you, raise a family with you and grow old with you. I love you with all my heart, Meagan. Will you marry me and be my wife?"

He opened the box and presented it for her to see. It contained a pure white diamond in a platinum setting. Surrounding the main stone were eight pieces of black hematite faceted to look like glittering black diamonds. It was the most beautiful ring she had ever seen. She raised her head to look at him as tears began streaming down her face.

"Oh, David, how can I possibly refuse? I have loved you all my life because I have dreamed of finding a man like you all my life. And then you stepped out of my dream and became real. I am the luckiest woman in the world to have you love me. Yes, David, I will gladly marry you."

He placed the ring on her finger and she threw her arms around him and kissed him. Her tears of happiness had both faces damp.

"Can we dispense with the mushy part now?" asked Jerry as he and Carolyn walked up. Both had tears on their faces as well. "I guess congratulations are in order." He hugged David then turned to Meagan and kissed her tenderly. Carolyn gave both of them a hug and kiss and wished them well.

David had told the Claytons of his plans to propose to Meagan at the Seven Glaciers. They had remained out of sight during the meal then followed the two outdoors. The two couples returned to the restaurant and a waiting table. A bottle of Dom Perignon arrived with four glasses. Jerry raised his glass and proposed a toast. "To David and Meagan. May the happiest days of your past be the saddest of your future." Glasses clinked against each other and they sipped their champagne.

"So when is the big date?" asked Carolyn.

"We haven't set one yet," replied David. "I was only concerned at this point with having her say yes."

"It was a foregone conclusion on her part. I knew it the moment I first met her. We only had to wait for you to come to your senses."

"It took me a while but I got there."

"I'm glad for both of you. I know you'll have a long, loving life together filled with a great deal of happiness."

They chatted amiably together for the next half hour. They then took the tram back down to the resort. David had made arrangements for he and Meagan to spend the night while the Claytons were heading back to Homer. They retrieved their suitcases and checked in.

Their room was located on the top floor of the hotel and the windows provided breathtaking views of the surrounding mountains. They performed their nighttime ablations and climbed into bed. She looked again in amazement at the ring on her finger. Her dreams were all coming true.

After breakfast the following morning they drove back to Homer. As they were passing the Kenai Princess Lodge she asked him to turn in. Once they had parked she went inside to the gift shop and purchased a pouch identical to the one she wore around her neck. When they returned to the car she took her pouch off and took out the small stone heart. She placed it in the new pouch and fastened it around David's neck.

"I think this heart is supposed to be yours now. Or should I say it is yours again. I'm not sure which describes it better. I only know I'm supposed to return it to you."

ABOUT THE AUTHOR

J. Michael Herron is the pen name used by Mike Herron. Black Diamonds is his first novel and the first in his planned Colors of Alaska Trilogy. He originally thought he would write a mystery or thriller but once he started to compose his thoughts he found himself drawn to writing a modern day love story. His niche is bringing legends and love to life.

While touring Alaska for four months in their 5th wheel he and his wife Susan fell in love with the Kenai Peninsula and Homer. Their son came to visit them and ended up moving to Homer. The couple now lives in the North Georgia Mountains.

Email him at: jmichael@2herrons.com

You can follow him and learn more about his books on either his Facebook page or his blog.

www.facebook.com/JMichaelHerron

www.jmichaelherron.blogspot.com

And please take the time to write a review on Amazon.com

19113010R00185

Made in the USA
Charleston, SC
07 May 2013